Books should be returned on or before the
last date stamped below

Marie and Mary

By the same author

Nigel Tranter

Marie and Mary

Hodder & Stoughton

Copyright © 2004 Frances May Baker

First published in Great Britain in 2004 by Hodder and Stoughton
A division of Hodder Headline

1 3 5 7 9 10 8 6 4 2

A CIP catalogue record for this title is available from
the British Library

ISBN 0 340 82354 2

Typeset in Sabon by Phoenix Typesetting,
Auldgirth, Dumfriesshire

Printed and bound in Great Britain by
Mackays of Chatham Ltd, Chatham, Kent

Hodder Headline's policy is to use papers that are natural, renewable and
recyclable products and made from wood grown in sustainable forests. The
logging and manufacturing processes are expected to conform to the environ-
mental regulations of the country of origin

Hodder and Stoughton
A division of Hodder Headline
338 Euston Road
London NW1 3BH

Principal Characters
In order of appearance

Marie de Guise: Sister of the Duke of Guise of France.

Claude, Duke of Guise: Eldest brother of above.

Charles of Guise, Cardinal of Lorraine: Younger brother.

François d' Orléans, Duke of Longueville: Kinsman of the royal house of France.

François, or Francis: Child of the duke and Marie; duke in his turn.

King James the Fifth: King of Scots.

Sir Andrew Wood of Largo: Admiral of Scotland.

Lord Maxwell: Powerful Scots Borders noble.

Elizabeth: Wife of Sir Andrew Wood.

Cardinal David Beaton: Archbishop of St Andrews.

James Stewart, Duke of Rothesay: Infant of Marie and the king.

Oliver Sinclair: Young laird of Whitekirk, in East Lothian.

Thomas Howard, Duke of Norfolk: Great Marshal of England.

Mary Queen of Scots: Child of Marie de Guise.

James Hamilton, Earl of Arran: Great Scots noble, with royal links.

James Douglas, Earl of Angus: Lieutenant-General of Scotland.

Henry the Eighth: Tudor King of England.

Sir David Lindsay of the Mount: Lord Lyon King of Arms, in Scotland.

Mary Fleming: Daughter of the Lord Fleming. One of the queen's Marys.

John Knox: Protestant divine.

Edward Seymour, Earl of Hertford: Regent in England.

Archibald Campbell, Earl of Argyll: Great Scots noble. Vice-Chancellor.

George Gordon, Earl of Huntly: Chancellor of Scotland.

John MacDonald of Moidart: Powerful Highland chief, known as Clanranald.

Andrew Wood, Younger of Largo: son of above.

Sir Ralph Sadler: English envoy.

D'Oysel: French envoy.

Henry Sinclair: Dean of Glasgow.

Lord Home: Powerful Borders noble. Warden of the East March.

Sir William Maitland of Lethington: Scottish Secretary of State.

Sir William Kirkcaldy of Grange: Noted soldier.

Catherine de Medici: Queen of France.

Elizabeth Tudor: Queen of England. Daughter of Henry the Eighth.

William Cecil, Lord Burghley: English statesman.

Erskine of Dun: Strong Protestant laird.

James Hepburn, Earl of Bothwell: Powerful Scots noble. Lord High Admiral.

James Stewart, Earl of Moray: Illegitimate son of James the Fifth.

Sir John Gordon: Second son of the Earl of Huntly.

Henry Stewart, Lord Darnley: Eldest son of the Earl of Lennox.

David Rizzio: Italian musician and poet at the Scottish court.

Sir Thomas Kerr of Ferniehirst: Borders magnate.

Lord Borthwick: Powerful Scottish noble.

James Stewart, Duke of Rothesay: Infant son of the queen. Later James the Sixth.

Lord Seton: Lothians noble. Father of one of the Marys.

Will Douglas: Son of the Keeper of Loch Leven Castle.

Lord Claud Hamilton: Son of the Duke of Chatelherault.

John Maxwell, Lord Herries: West March magnate.

Lord Knollys: English noble.

Elizabeth, Lady Cavendish: Wife of Sir William. Known as Bess of Hardwicke.

Robert Devereux, Earl of Essex: Favourite of Queen Elizabeth of England.

Sir Amyas Paulet: English courtier.

Sir Francis Walsingham: English Secretary of State.

Part One

I

The young woman looked at her two elder brothers, exasperated. "Why Longueville?" she demanded. "He is old enough to be my father. He has had two wives already. No children by either, both dying in childbirth. Is that a good recommendation for me? And Longue is far away, far beyond Paris. When I marry, I would choose my own husband!"

"We know of your interest in young D'Arcis," her eldest brother said. "But such as he is not for the likes of you. Longueville is a duke and related to the royal house, a D'Orléans. It would be a suitable match for a Guise. And you, Marie, I would remind you, are not in a position to decide who you would wed."

"I am nineteen!" she asserted. "Not to be married off to whom *you* choose, Claude!"

"You will do as we say," the Duke of Guise told her. "Longueville it is. We have discussed it well, and so chosen."

"He is none so ill," the other brother, Charles, said. "Our two dukedoms, allied, will serve France well, and King Francis. Be not so stubborn, Marie. We know what is best."

"What do you, a churchman, know about marriage? A cardinal you may be, but that does not make you understand women and their feelings and wishes, does it?"

Marie de Guise was a comely, well-built creature, tall,

fair, pleasingly rounded, characterful, and knowing her own mind. Her younger brothers were well aware of this, all seven of them, and heedful not unduly to cross her, although she was warm-hearted and nowise exacting in manner. She had run this household of Châteaudun since their mother had died four years before, quite a responsibility for a fifteen-year-old. But these two elder ones, Claude, Duke of Guise, and Charles, Cardinal of Lorraine, used to rule and governance in state and Church, were concerned to maintain their authority, the Guises being one of the greatest families of all France.

"Longueville and Guise will make a worthy alliance," Claude declared. "He is agreeable . . ."

"Agreeable to marry, perhaps; but not agreeable as a husband for *me*! Have I no say in the matter?"

"You will find him well enough, girl. You met him, three years ago, is it? Before his last wife died. We have spoken with him, at Paris. He will come here and take you in marriage in due course. It is arranged. Say you no more about it."

And that was that. The dukedoms of France were apt to be associated thus. Marie shook her fair head, but recognised that she would probably have to make the best of it, whatever her feelings towards Charles D'Arcis. Such was life.

François d'Orléans, Duke of Longueville, duly arrived at Châteaudun a couple of weeks later, having had to ride a long way with his escort of men for Longue was fully three hundred miles to the south-west, in the Loire valley, with Paris in between. He was a large and massive man, with a shock of greying hair and beard and a masterful manner. Marie recognised that he was sizing her up with entirely evident calculation, and, she later complained to her younger brothers, almost as though she had been a cow at a market, assessing her shape and lineaments, so that she felt that perhaps she ought to turn around on her heels and display her rear view also for inspection. He seemed to be the sort of man who would put a large value on physical matters and proportions. At least he made no complaints at what he saw; she almost wished that he would do so, for she was less than enamoured of him, and would have rather welcomed rejection. He had hot eyes under those bristling eyebrows. He had viewed her before, but that was while she was still not fully of womanly maturity. Distinctly physically basic as he might be, it did occur to her to wonder why both his wives had died in childbirth. That was a somewhat worrying thought. Could she use this as a means of persuading her brothers that becoming the third Duchess of Longueville might not be advantageous?

She had to act hostess to the man, and would no doubt be judged on that front also.

When it came for his departure, however, all seemed to have been arranged, she not being consulted. He announced that they would wed in six weeks' time, at Notre-Dame in Paris, as more convenient for his family and friends than having to come to the châteaux area. This evidently was his attitude to life.

The six weeks passed all too swiftly for Marie. Then it was Paris for her and her brothers.

François had brought surprisingly few family and friends to the wedding – or perhaps these were just getting tired of attending such. Or it might be that he had not invited them, possibly in short supply anyway. The Guises and their friends greatly outnumbered the rest.

Marie kept reminding herself that weddings were

supposed to be joyful occasions – which was not in any way what she felt.

The ceremony and feasting over, the bridegroom announced to her that he had a town-house near the church of St Eustache. Thence they were bound, without delay.

Indeed, bride and groom were barely inside the premises when François grasped Marie, all but lifting her off her feet, well-built as she was, and pushed her, past the staring servants, up to a bedchamber on the first floor, where he planted her on the bed and began to drag off her fine clothing, careless as to what might tear, this with no spoken accompaniment but with grunts and heavy breathing, whatever her protests. Near naked as no matter, he flung himself upon her. Devastated, she found herself being raped by this huge man, large in all ways.

It became, for her, a chaos of affright, distress and pain, as she was crushed down under his weight and his heaving, panting person. Gasping for breath, she sought to shut off her mind from what was happening, this less than success-fully. And she was now married to this!

It did not go on for very long – not this first time, at any rate. He rolled off her, and was snoring in moments. She lay there, eyes shut, wishing that her mind and conscious-ness were shut also, hating the feeling and awareness of her own body.

She must have drifted off to sleep of a sort, despite her revulsion, when she was rudely awakened by the man clambering over her once more. Was he not satisfied? Apparently not.

This time it took longer, and was the worse, more heaving and thrusting and panting. So this was being Duchess of Longueville!

The man further used her before he lay back, and his breathing became more regular. Dare she hope . . . ?

So commenced Marie's life with François d'Orléans, if life it could be called. She had come to loathe the man, and all to do with him, and she reproved herself for so feeling; after all, had she not sworn marriage vows? Fortunately he was often away, for he had many estates, and visited them frequently – and blessedly saw no need to take her with him. No doubt he had other women available at them all.

It was only a few months before she realised that she was pregnant. So she was to become mother as well as wife. When she told him, he said that he wanted no more deaths in childbirth, and that it had better be a son. His dukedom needed an heir. But her condition did not stop him using her. That was the way it was, love and caring not involved. She just had to put up with him.

The weeks passed, Marie a tested young woman.

More testing when it came to her time for delivery. As first births go, it was perhaps not a difficult one, but it was no physically enjoyable event nevertheless, as she laboured for those hours. But when at last she looked down on the little round face and blue eyes which the midwife presented to her, she knew a surge of sheerest joy. Here, at last, someone to love and be loved by, her own, her very own, part of her yet a completely new creature; admittedly François's son, but somehow so utterly different and distinct from that great bear of a man that she could not associate him with the father. She would call him, not François, as no doubt the father would demand, but Francis. She whispered to herself that she had produced love personified.

Her husband welcomed an heir, however many bastards

7

he had fathered. He commanded celebrations and rejoicings on a great scale throughout the dukedom, bonfires to be lit, feasting to be held, and the infant to be taken all round the estates and paraded for tributes to be paid, Marie being more or less ignored, the child *his*, her part in it all scarcely recognised. Indeed he dispensed with her company on many of these demonstrations, wet-nurses adequate for the occasion as attendants.

The baby did much travelling in the weeks after his birth, carried in a kind of cradle slung between two pack-horses, for the Longueville properties were far-flung. And it so happened that from one of the most distant of these, only little Francis and his women carers came home to the unwanted Marie. The duke, careering over rocky ground in proud fashion, had been thrown from his horse as it stumbled and, crashing on a boulder, broke his neck.

The infant who was brought back to his mother was now Duke of Longueville.

Marie, now a widow in her twenty-second year, was less than stricken by mourning. Scarcely able to comprehend her situation fully, she fairly quickly removed herself from Longue, with her baby, to head home for the Guise house of Châteaudun and her brothers' company, a free woman.

In time she was able to put the nightmare of her marriage behind her, choosing not even to call herself Duchess of Longueville, although proud for little Francis to be called duke. She took over the running of the castle once again, as she had done since her mother's death; and soon it became as though those intervening years had never been. Francis was her joy. The family looked after the Longueville dukedom for her and their nephew, taking it in turns to reside on the various distant estates, these a source of great wealth. As well that she had so many brothers.

Life became acceptable and fulfilling.

Charles of Guise, the cardinal, took an especial interest in young Francis. Indeed he almost bewailed the fact that the infant was already a duke, or he would have sought to make another churchman out of him.

2

The Guise family frequently attended the royal court at Paris; and it was on one such occasion, when indeed they had been specially invited, that they met the King of Scots, James the Fifth, this at the town-palace of the Duke of Vendôme, a Bourbon, kin to King Francis. He had come to wed Marie de Bourbon, the duke's daughter; and great was the company gathered to celebrate the marriage.

But the Scots monarch, a good-looking, gallant and lively young man, was causing some concern to his hosts. For despite the proposed bride's evident approval of him, he was proving to be much more interested in the Princess Madeleine, the sixteen-year-old daughter of King Francis, very beautiful but delicately frail. The chosen Bourbon bride was manifestly upset by this. Marie de Guise and her brothers were intrigued by the situation, although King Francis clearly was not.

What went on thereafter between the two monarchs was unclear. But it presently became evident that King James was a man of determination, and not only knew his own mind but intended to have his own way. Poor Marie de Bourbon was rejected and dejected. Young Madeleine's father was requested to let her become the Queen of Scotland.

In the circumstances King Francis more or less had to concede.

So the marriage took place, after only a short interval, in the great cathedral of Notre-Dame, but not with the originally suggested bride, in the presence of two other monarchs, the Kings of France and Navarre, and no fewer than seven cardinals.

Marie de Guise commiserated with her Bourbon namesake, but was sufficiently romantically minded to recognise love at first sight. She liked James Stewart, and hoped that he would make a good husband to Madeleine.

Along with a great and distinguished company they saw the newly-weds board the Scots vessel, the *Yellow Caravel*, a handsome ship commanded by the Scots Admiral Sir Andrew Wood. It all made a dramatic and memorable occasion.

They heard in due course that the new queen had been warmly received in Scotland, especially when it was known that on landing at Leith, the port of Edinburgh, the capital, she had knelt on the ground and kissed the Scots soil, a touching gesture. King James was a proud and delighted man and the Auld Alliance with France was thus joyfully renewed.

Marie wished the royal couple well. But she had noted that Madeleine had been racked with coughing a number of times, once bringing up blood. She feared, she feared . . .

For herself she was happy with young Francis, a laughing, healthy boy, ever active and demanding of her attentions. She was able to forget his father.

Only a matter of months after James returned to Scotland with his bride, the news reached France. Madeleine had died. Her coughing had been indicative of a grievous ailment.

The king was devastated. Marie's fears had not been groundless. Two nations mourned. And Scotland still lacked an heir to the throne.

It was this requirement, together with the need to cement

the league with France to counter Henry Tudor's aggressions, which brought James Stewart back across the Channel none so long thereafter. And to Marie's astonishment, it was to see *her*. Apparently he had been impressed with her, in some degree, when he had come wooing Madeleine. Now, a French match seemingly still important, he had remembered her, a duchess, and her mother a Bourbon. He came to propose marriage. She had proved that she could mother a son. Now he, and Scotland, desired that heir to the throne. It was as simple as that. Would she wed him and become Queen of Scotland?

However surprised, Marie did not take long to make up her mind. She had liked James Stewart from the first. And she recognised that she needed a husband; also a father-figure for young Francis. She could scarcely do better than this. It was not that she particularly desired to be a queen. But if she remarried into her own caste, as it were, to some other duke, then the Longueville duchy might well become absorbed and downgraded, to the hurt of her Francis. This was unlikely to happen if she became queen of another realm.

She told James that she would wed him, yes.

It made a strange situation. There was no question of love between them, he still mourning his adored Madeleine; she having hated her previous marriage. She was unsure as to her physical reactions after that first experience. But if wed she should be, this probably was as good a joining as any. What sort of a queen would she make? And would those Scots accept her? They were said to be a fierce and quarrelsome lot, with their clans and feuds and Celtic pride.

James had to hasten back to his own realm, where he was having trouble with the powerful Douglases under the

Earl of Angus, former husband of Queen Margaret Tudor, the king's mother and Henry of England's sister, she no help to her son. He announced that he would send Sir Andrew Wood, the admiral, to fetch her to Scotland in his ship in due course.

So Marie had some weeks to prepare herself for this second bout of matrimony, which she trusted would be more successful than the first. It would have been good if she could have married for love; but that seemed not to be for the likes of herself. Affection had to be concentrated on young Francis.

A remarkable development arose shortly thereafter. An English envoy arrived at Châteaudun. Henry Tudor, that much married monarch, had recently lost his fourth wife, Jane Seymour, who had died in childbirth. He had apparently heard that his rival of Scotland was planning to marry Marie de Guise. Now he sent this ambassador to offer his hand instead, remarking on her suitability to be a queen, her excellent looks and stature, and her proven ability to bear sons. To be Queen of England would surely be much preferable to marrying James Stewart of modest Scotland.

Marie, however surprised, had no difficulty in rejecting this odd proposal. She sent the envoy back with a letter declaring that although her figure might be large enough for King Henry, her neck was small – this an oblique reference to the execution of Anne Boleyn, the Tudor's second wife and sister-in-law, married after the divorce of Queen Catherine of Aragon.

James, whether to demonstrate his preferable attitude to women and marriage compared with King Henry's or otherwise, sent a formal marriage-contract on 6 January 1538, the Day of the Epiphany; and a declaration that in

May his representative, the Lord Maxwell, would come to act bridegroom-by-proxy, and thereafter bring her to Scotland in notable style for the full nuptials at St Andrew's Cathedral.

This all seemed very formal and correct, but presumably how royal marriages were arranged in Scotland.

Marie had had three months to prepare to become queen of a realm she knew nothing about, a land reputedly consisting of mountains, lakes, wild animals and wilder men – although this James seemed nowise wild compared with her former French husband. Her brothers declared that the Scots did not know either what was coming to them!

There was, however, a grievous parting. Her mother, the Duchess Antoinette, convinced her that young Francis should be left behind in her keeping. To take the child of a previous marriage to her new husband's kingdom would be most inadvisable, and look odd to the Scots. Let the boy remain with her meantime.

James did not come himself to conduct her to his kingdom, but sent a sufficiency of representatives, two thousand of them, under his friend the Lord Maxwell, lords, knights and churchmen, with Admiral Wood in his fleet, all presumably to emphasise the importance of the occasion; and possibly to remind his unloved mother, Margaret Tudor, that there was to be a new queen.

When this vast contingent arrived in Paris, even the great cathedral of Notre-Dame was crowded out for the rather odd ceremony of marriage-by-proxy, Marie seemingly being wed to Lord Maxwell, who already had a wife.

Not feeling, thereafter, in the least wifely, much less a queen, it crossed Marie's mind to wonder what the Lady

Maxwell thought of all this. Also, even if only at the back of her mind, whether the said lord might assume that his proxy-ship gave him the right to spend this curious wedding night with the bride.

However, Maxwell was correctness and discretion personified. At the banquet, which the Guise brothers laid on to celebrate, he made a brief speech declaring his pride and appreciation at being honoured thus to serve his liege-lord, and his respect and admiration for his new sovereign-lady.

Marie passed a wedding night of a sort alone in her bed, young Francis, whom she would have to leave behind on the morrow, sleeping nearby.

There was no delay thereafter, Marie in tears as she had to hand her son to her mother. She was conducted to the ships in the Seine, where she embarked, all the great company to be carried in half a dozen other of the admiral's craft for the voyage downriver to the Norse Sea and northwards.

Marie found herself attended by a lady-in-waiting, none other than Elizabeth, Lady Wood, wife of the admiral, a pleasing person with whom she got on well, and who had helped to look after young Francis. Presumably James had arranged this, although she learned that Elizabeth frequently accompanied her husband on his many voyages.

On the tenth day of June, in fine weather, they crossed the mouth of the Firth of Forth, passing close to an isolated but quite large island called the May, to land at the fishing harbour of Crail, this one year after the late Madelaine had done the same.

Marie was already impressed by the views. She had heard that Scotland was famed for its dramatic scenery, not only the mountains and isles, its forests, glens and heather. As they sailed up she had noted the towering cliffs and headlands, the yawning caves and castle-crowned pinnacles. Now she saw the vast rock-stack, its sheer sides white with the droppings of the wheeling myriad of seafowl, which she was told was the Craig of Bass, with a conical summit behind, and great green ranges of hills stretching out of sight to the south. That was Lothian, Lady Wood informed. Now, ahead, this Fife was different, only isolated hills, not extended heights, smaller cliffs, many fishing havens of whitewashed houses with red-tiled roofs, little woodland and much cattle country.

This Crail appeared to be the last of the fisherfolk communities before the great thrusting headland projecting proudly into the Norse Sea, which Elizabeth told her was called Fife Ness, ness meaning a promontory. It was none so far from their destination, which was St Andrews, the ecclesiastical capital of the land, where King James would be awaiting them.

They came round to this, a town of spires and steeples innumerable, with a great abbey and many priories and monastic houses; also a university with its colleges. This did not sound like the wild country she had been told about.

Landed, Marie was led to the abbey, where James received her, with a host of clerics, but also the provost and bailies of the town, the equivalent of her French mayors and councillors, with local lords and landowners. He greeted her with a hearty kiss and, looking her up and down frankly, seemed pleased with what he saw, and kissed her again. She accepted his salutations smilingly, and decided that he was even better than she had remembered him, which was a comforting thought, since she was now wed to him by proxy.

The large company paraded through the streets, these thronged with cheering folk, James bowing right and left and waving a hand. Obviously he was a popular monarch. They halted here and there, to receive gifts of flowers and sweetmeats; whether this had been arranged by James, or was a spontaneous welcome to the new queen, she did not know. But she received them as graciously as she might, before handing them over to Maxwell's ready attendants.

There were set pageants and displays at various points along their roundabout route, with choirs and instrumentalists to greet them, all very different from Marie's previous notions of Scottish folk and behaviour; she realised how ignorant she had been. It looked as though she was going to enjoy being queen to these people, whatever it was like being married to their king.

At the archepiscopal palace they were greeted by Cardinal David Beaton, head of the Church in Scotland and, she understood, the first Scot to reach that status. He was a tall, slender man in his early forties, quite fine of feature with a small pointed beard and an authoritative stance, son of a Fife laird. Marie had already met him briefly in France, when he had for a time acted as Bishop of Mirapoix before his translation to cardinalship, introduced by her own brother, Cardinal Charles of Lorraine. He was to conduct the final nuptials, and he joined the procession to the cathedral.

There this prolonged marriage ceremonial was at last ended, the public part of it at least, and in splendid style, the large ecclesiastical premises being sufficiently capacious to hold all the congregation. Marie de Guise was, for better or worse, finally made Queen of Scotland.

Back at the cardinal's palace, the wedding feast was more than adequate for the occasion, with speeches and

17

varied entertainment. At James's side, Marie saw that he was growing impatient. Was he so eager for the next stage in this day's or night's, proceedings? For herself, she wondered and wondered. Would she disappoint? Or be disappointed? What was she hoping for indeed?

At length, with a second performance of gypsy acrobats being announced, the king rose, as therefore must all. Taking Marie's arm, he thanked Beaton, on his left, for all his major contributions to the day.

The cardinal, smiling, waved to Lord Maxwell to preside meantime, and led the royal couple from the dais platform, by its rear door, and upstairs, conducting them to the suite of three rooms in a flanking tower. Female servants awaited them here, with hot water for ablutions, and more wine and sweetmeats. With tactful expressions of goodwill and for a rewarding night, the cardinal left them there.

James asked Marie whether she required the further services of the women, and at her shake of the head, he dismissed them.

Alone at last, he turned to her. "Here is a trying situation for you, no? For myself also, perhaps. We have both been wed before, and come to such night. And now it is, shall we say, for state advantage? I recognise your woman's position. It may well be that you are . . . reluctant. Man and wife we may be, but I would not wish to force myself upon you too soon. How say you?"

Marie searched his face. "You are . . . kind," she said. "I, I thank you for your caring in this. You suggest that, this night, we . . . separate?"

"If so it would best please you. I sought, and obtained, these three rooms. One for your small son. One for you, if . . . ?"

"How would *you* have it, James?"

"I would have you to choose, Marie. I give you time."

"Time? Will time make any difference? I am now yours. And I judge that you will be sufficiently gentle!" She bit her lip. "And I would have you to know that I *liked* you, found you pleasing from our first meeting."

"And I you. So? We share a room and a bed, then, this night?"

She nodded.

He walked a pace or two and back. "Then, may I have the pleasure of undressing you?"

"Why not? If it will give you the more satisfaction."

"From the looks of you, woman, I judge that it will! You are notably well endowed, my dear."

"Your dear? Then so be it." And she raised her arms wide, in offering.

He went to her then, into those arms, and flung his own around her, kissing. And quickly those kisses grew the warmer, more urgent, and his hands began to caress and stroke and search. She shivered. But it was not with cold nor mislike but in a sort of womanly appreciative reaction. For Marie de Guise was all woman.

When her lips stirred and opened under his, he all but shook her, panting incoherences.

Soon she was panting also, moreover aiding his busy hands at the removal of her clothing, indeed their arms interlocking and hindering, to her incipient laughter and his head-shaking frustration.

When her last undergarment fell to the floor and she stood naked in all her ripe and rounded femininity, James stood back to survey, deep-breathing, gazing his head shaking once again, but in far from frustration. In all but wonder indeed, for she made a sight to see for any man in the candlelight. From kind eyes and fair hair falling on wide shoulders, to large swelling breasts, down to not ungenerous stomach and the dark V of her loins, all above shapely thighs and long legs.

He shook his head now, wordless. And on impulse, she swung round to present her rear view to him also, telling herself that she ought to be ashamed of herself, but laughing as she did so. She had not realised that she could be so earthly-minded. But James's admiration and acclaim was so obvious as to make all self-questioning vanish. She even stepped forward now, to meet him, as he flung himself upon her once more.

Had she been a sylph-like creature he would no doubt have carried her bodily over to the bed. As it was, he did not actually have to drag her thither, but impelled her, she protesting – but only that he was still fully clad while she was not. Sitting on the covers, she sought to aid him to undress, but found this of little avail in his twistings and bendings. Getting those boots off was the major trouble.

His shirt still on, he clambered beside her, and then abruptly halted, to search her face there in the dim light, holding her.

"You, you are willing?" he demanded. "It is not just me? My, my need. I would not have it so. Woman, say that you would have me! Say it, of a mercy!"

"Need I?" she asked. "Would I be thus, foolish one? Naked, and your wife. But, but . . . be not over-hasty, husband. I, I . . . !" She got out no more.

"I will seek to serve you. And myself, to our good. Our satisfaction. Dear woman!"

No more words, only motion and panting and murmuring, as she spread herself for him and he entered her person. In fact gentle he could not be, but he sought to be less than hasty, controlling himself as best he could, with Marie over-tense. She could not help remembering the last time she had been in this situation, or at least some likeness of it, and it had been hateful. Now it was not to be, she told herself.

And, after the first minute or two, it was not, and her breathings and gasps were sighs of thankfulness.

James was driven by male exactions and demands, seeking delay as he would. Now it was his turn to endeavour the not-to-be, not yet, not yet . . .

But physical imperatives overcame mental solicitude, and Marie was left less than fulfilled, as he cried out and reached *his* climax, she shaking her head as he heaved and groaned over her.

He recognised that he had failed her, and vowed, promised, reiterated thickly his assurance that he would do better for her shortly, she doubting.

But he was right. With no lengthy delay, he was all man again. And this time for long enough to enable her to become all woman indeed. Mutual satisfaction achieved, a king and queen could sink back to sleep in royal gratification.

Love had taken the place of mere esteem and liking.

That was just the beginning of it. Forty days and forty nights they spent based at St Andrews, visiting the country-side all around, especially Falkland, the royal hunting-palace much favoured by James; climbing the Lomond Hills nearby, as well as Largo Law, and the lesser heights of Lindifferon and Tarvit and Rhind, and viewing the magnificent prospects therefrom; of all of which James was proud. He told Marie of the varied and very different parts of his kingdom: the Borderland with its dales and hills, and its mosstroopers in the Debateable Land; Lothian across Forth, with its dramatic coastline and the capital city; the Tay which they had viewed, and the north-east from Dundee right up to Aberdeen and Inverness; the far north, to the Pentland Firth, with the Orkneys and Shetlands beyond; the western Highlands and Isles, so vast and beautiful with their great mountains and sea lochs; the Clyde estuary and Glasgow; Arran and the Ayrshire coast; and Galloway, all but a kingdom of its own. All this he would take her to see, in due course.

Marie found it all fascinating and much to her taste. She liked the people, independent of mind, anything but obsequious, yet friendly, clearly approving of their monarch. She was determined that they should approve of her also, a Frenchwoman.

As well as viewing the land, visiting the lords and lairds and clerics, the villages and towns, there were innumerable occasions to attend, pageants, games, contests, joustings, minstrelsy, dancing in the streets, some of it arranged by James himself but much spontaneous, a people's greeting to their new queen, and as such warmly appreciated.

Winter was almost upon them, and wider travel would have to be postponed, especially to the highlands, with the passes apt to be blocked by snow. But some of the cities could be visited.

First, it must be the capital. Sailing from Fife in one of Sir Andrew Wood's ships, they docked at Leith. Horses took them up the two miles to Edinburgh, this under the majestic lion-like isolated hill, all but a mountain, called Arthur's Seat, relating to some earlier monarch, James told her. Other heights rose all around, Scotland indeed living up to its reputation in this respect at least.

They made a triumphal entry to the capital, greeted by the provost and his bailies, with more welcoming revelry and street entertainment, even though a thin, misty rain began to fall and cloaks were in order. Cheering crowds were so dense that outriders had difficulty in clearing a passage for the royal party. They were bound for the Abbey of the Holy Rood, the abbot's princely house there, a more suitable lodging for the new queen than the great rock-top citadel which vied with Arthur's Seat in dominating the city.

Still further entertainment, with feasting, was provided for all, Marie beginning to fear that she was going to suffer indigestion if this generous hospitality continued. But she had no doubts as to her welcome. Bedding down with James that night, she was well assured that she was going to be more than content with her new homeland.

3

Marie was not disappointed. That winter, wet and chilly as it was, left her amply assured. However much of an arranged marriage it had been, she had made no mistake in coming to Scotland. James proved to be a kind and undemanding husband, and her duties as queen gave her considerable satisfaction. There were rumours that James had a mistress at Tantallon Castle, a Douglas stronghold to the east of Edinburgh, but that was only to be expected of a monarch wed for state advantage.

Although the king had to be based mainly at Edinburgh, they were much at Stirling Castle, where Marie could view the Highland Line of blue mountains which she liked; also at Falkland where, a good horsewoman, she soon learned to enjoy hunting deer on the Lomond Hills. James taught her the sport of archery, with both longbow and crossbow, at which she became efficient, even outdoing her husband. A favourite haunt was Duddingston Loch, at the south side of Edinburgh's Arthur's Seat, where there were flocks of duck and a few heron. Although hawking was the usual sport here, Marie learned to shoot duck with the crossbow, fast-flying as they were. Aim two ducks ahead of a duck was the secret. The fowl, when hit, were apt to fall into the water, so dogs had to be used to retrieve them. The queen, riding from Holyrood Abbey round the hill with her dogs, became quite a common sight for the Edinburgh folk.

The king often took her with him on his many royal

duties in the Lothians, the Borders and over to Glasgow and the west, as well as to St Andrews in Fife. She got to know all southern Scotland fairly well. The Highlands and the Isles ever beckoned her, however, from Stirling, and James promised that they should go and explore there just as soon as was possible and the mountain passes negotiable, for he had boasted of them, the most scenic and exciting area of all his kingdom.

The plan was for them to ride north from Stirling, by Perth and the great Forest of Atholl, forest referring in this case to *deer*-forest, not trees, this right to the River Spey, and over to Elgin, Nairn and Inverness. There one of Sir Andrew Wood's ships would pick them up, sail them past the less scenic counties of moor and pasture and bog, and round the Pentland Firth to the Hebrides and the West Highland coast, there to enjoy, search and visit. August it should be for that.

Meanwhile she played the queen as best she could.

August came, and James did not delay, especially as Marie declared that she believed herself to be pregnant.

Marie greatly enjoyed that journey, all of it. They had mountains in France, of course, but somehow these were different, probably not rising so high, but fiercer-seeming, more colourful in more than their heather covering and cascading white waterfalls; great herds of red deer drifted like cloud-shadows over the steep slopes, and eagles could be glimpsed, hovering high.

They halted overnight at the castles of the Drummonds, Murrays and Stewarts; and once over the great Pass of Dumochter and down into Speyside, at those of the clan chiefs of Macpherson and Mackintosh, Forbes and Fraser and Brodie, where Marie met a different sort of lord, tartan-clad and soft-spoken, proud without being haughty, their clansmen treated like kinsfolk rather than retainers.

Marie loved the Highlands and their people, even though James was not always sure of their fealty, they tending to have different allegiances and priorities.

They left the mountains at Aviemore, to follow the great River Spey eastwards, although the heights loomed ever blue on either side, more distant. They were heading for Elgin, where James wished to see the Bishop of Moray at his palace of Spynie, a powerful cleric who, he hoped, could help in his relationship with the Highland chiefs.

From Spynie they rode west by south the fifty miles by the communities of Forres and Findhorn, Auldearn and Nairn, on the Moray Firth coast, and on by Ardersier and Culloden Moor to Inverness, the Highland capital. There they found Sir Andrew Wood duly awaiting them with his great ship, the *Yellow Caravel*; he was a quite elderly man of authoritative bearing but lively and with a sense of humour. He would take them to the Isles which James was so anxious to have Marie discover.

Sailing, she was interested in the Ross coastline north of Inverness, with its Cromarty and Dornoch Firths and its long peninsulas; but James said that these were as nothing, scenically, compared with where they were making for. Admittedly, the further north they went the less dramatic grew the shores, with modest cliffs backed by seemingly endless moors and lowish hills, this past the port of Wick and all the Sinclair country. Eventually they rounded Duncansby Head, the north-eastern tip of all Scotland, and into the Pentland Firth, which separated the mainland from the isles of Orkney and Shetland.

Marie asked about these last, which they could see distantly; for the theory was that the Guises were of Norman, that is Norseman, extraction, and these isles were said to be populated by folk whose forebears had come from Scandinavia. But James said that must await another occasion. The Hebrides and West Highland coasts would demand as much time as he could afford to be away from the tasks of ruling his realm.

Wood, the admiral, made good company, full of stories to tell of the areas they were passing.

The voyage along the Pentland Firth was longer than James had remembered, almost one hundred miles of it, passing the quite large town of Thurso, and innumerable headlands, with the sea lochs, or kyles, of Tongue, Eriboll and Durness, the scenery growing the more attractive as they progressed, mountains beginning to dominate the landscape. Eventually they came to the turning-point, Cape Wrath, thrusting out into the Atlantic like some great fist shaken in the face of the ocean, and Wood could turn his vessel southwards. He told them that Wrath was but a corruption of the Norse *hvarf*, which indeed meant turning-point. He was knowledgeable about such things.

Even now the Hebrides were still distant, although Lewis, the northernmost of the Outer Isles, soon became evident. They had fifty more miles to sail before they could be said to reach the Isles proper, the small group of the Summer Isles heralding the vast area of mountains, islands, peninsulas, sea lochs and kyles or narrows that constituted the Hebrides. Wood suggested that the name came from the words *heb eid*, meaning without corn, indicating the lack of arable land to be found there.

Thereafter she was enthralled by all that she saw, the challenge and colour and diversity of it, from the blue mountains, the dark ravines scoring their sides, the green pine trees and mosses, the multi-hued seaweeds decking the reefs and skerries, and the white cockleshell sand which, shining through the clear waters, reflected palest aquamarine and azure. Here was a wonderland indeed, beyond even her expectations. Marie praised God for it.

Four days they spent, after calling briefly at Tarbert of Harris, one of the Outer Isles, before sailing down to great Skye, the largest of the islands, only rivalled by Mull. James said that they should not land on any hereafter, time for him precious, and rivalry among the Highland chiefs as to visits being an issue to be avoided. Admittedly their vessel would be seen and reported on, the *Caravel* readily identified with its high fore- and after-castles and ranked gun-ports, but none would know that the monarch was aboard.

So after long Skye they sailed down by Rhum with its parasitical clouds atop its jagged mountains, Eigg with its thrusting Sgurr, a columnar peak at one end, the smaller Muck, the long mainland peninsula of Ardnamurchan of the MacIans, the smaller isles of Coll, Tiree and Colonsay, to great Mull, Jura with its twin breast-like hills and spreading Islay, all of which intrigued Marie with their remarkable beauty yet variety. James debated with Wood as to the attitudes and reliability towards the crown of their chiefs, and their alliances and feudings. This was something of a world unto itself, of MacDonalds, MacLeods, MacIans, Macleans, MacAulays, MacEwans and the rest. Marie listened, watched and wondered.

On and on, down to the lengthy promontory of Kintyre they went, and round its spectacular Mull into the wide Clyde estuary, to pass the huge island of Arran, this in order to reach the royal castle of Dumbarton, extraordinarily sited on top of a quite major hill rising directly from the waters. Here they landed, for the king to consult with its keeper, a son of the Earl of Lennox, another Stewart, before proceeding on to the city of Glasgow, where James had an archbishop to see, who was not always in agreement with Cardinal and Archbishop Beaton.

Marie was learning something of the problems and preoccupations of ruling an unruly kingdom.

They left Sir Andrew and the ship at Glasgow, borrowing horses to ride eastwards for Stirling, much more speedy than sailing all the way back to the east coast. James was a little concerned about Marie in the saddle in her pregnant state, but she assured him that there was no danger in it at this stage. Childbearing, after all, was not a new experience for her.

She wondered daily how her little Duke Francis was faring with his grandmother.

4

Marie was duly brought to bed and delivered of a son, an heir to the throne of Scotland, to great rejoicing, this in the May of 1540. He was to be one more James. The king made a proud father, and she an attentive mother to her second ducal offspring, this one Duke of Rothesay. Where was Rothesay? Her husband told her it was a small town with a large, ancient castle on the Isle of Bute in the Clyde estuary just north of Arran, Stewart country. It seemed a strange style for the Scots heir to the throne, but the fortress had been important to the High Stewards of Scotland, whence came the surname Stewart. Marie was learning.

The royal couple heard extraordinary news. King Henry of England was much disappointed that they had produced a boy. He had apparently hoped for a girl, to whom he would have sought to have his little son Edward betrothed, so that one day they would marry and this young man become wearer of the crown-matrimonial and king-consort of Scotland, and thus bring English domination over the northern kingdom nearer, ever the ambition of the southern monarchy.

The royal family spent much of their time at Falkland, in Fife, not only because James was so fond of hunting on the Lomond Hills, but on account of it being convenient of access for many parts of his realm: by ship from nearby Methil or Buckhaven where Admiral Wood of Largo kept his fleet, and so able to reach Edinburgh, the Borders coast, up Forth to Stirling, up Tay to Perth and Dundee, and so further north. Admittedly Glasgow, Ayrshire, Dumfries and Galloway were far off, but even a king could not have everything. Marie had no complaints to make; and although she much loved the Highland mountains and Isles, she realised that this was not an area from which to rule a nation. She showed her approval of Falkland by importing wild boars from France for more exciting hunting, and pear and plum trees for the palace orchard.

It was good for her to have a child to attend to, and play the mother as well as the enterprising queen.

James took her to see Rothesay, on an island easily reached by land, the Kyles of Bute crossed by ferry. The town clustered around the great castle, one of the most ancient in the land, built by Robert the Second in the thirteenth century on the site of a Pictish fort. It was very much circular, all its walls rounded save for a rectangular gatehouse, the lofty walling having four projecting towers and enclosing a courtyard, all gaunt and challenging, not the sort of place Marie would have chosen to give title to the royal heir. James admitted that he had never occupied it. Dumbarton, despite its perch-like site above the Clyde, was much more convenient and accessible. Why not change the child's title then? Marie asked. Make him Duke of Dumbarton? But that met with head-shaking. Traditions had to be maintained. If, then, she had another son, what was he to be styled? Duke of Ross, James declared, ever the second son's title. Ross seemed a far away area, and with no Stewart connection, but this presumably dated from the early Pictish times when the High Kings of Alba were based at Inverness.

Marie developed a strange anxiety, these days. She had

not worried unduly about her husband's interest in that Douglas young woman at Tantallon. But now he was, she judged, seeing too much of a young *male* friend, one Oliver Sinclair of Whitekirk in Haddingtonshire, and he was very secretive about this. He was friendly with many of his lords, of course; but this seemed different, an almost furtive association, Sinclair never invited to court events nor to Marie's presence, yet James often made excuses to visit that Haddington area. When she asked about this individual, James brushed it off and changed the subject. It was somewhat worrying.

Over-soon, whatever the king's concerns elsewhere, he had Marie with child again. In early 1541 the queen gave birth to a second Stewart son, whom they named Robert. James, learning that the powerful Highland Earl of Ross much objected to any prince being styled duke thereof, agreed to change the projected title to Duke of Albany, a suitable reference to the child's descent from the ancient Albannach kings. So Scotland seemed assured of the royal succession.

Sadly indeed the rejoicing changed to grief, for the new prince died only days later; and more direly still, whether by some infection or otherwise, the little brother James of Rothesay choked to death also.

Devastated, Marie wept. But she nevertheless found the strength to comfort James who, as well as having lost his little sons saw his realm again without any direct heir to the throne, she telling him that they were both young enough yet to expect to produce more children, this despite her deep grieving.

The king was not to be consoled. He declared that it was God's judgment on his sins. Apparently he had had a terrible dream. Sir James Hamilton of Finnart, an illegitimate son of the Earl of Arran, a scoundrel who had murdered the Earl of Lennox and was even said to be plotting the monarch's own death, and who James had had executed, came to him in his sleep, and told him that he would lose both his arms and finally his royal head.

Low in spirits, it was strange that it was to Oliver Sinclair that the king turned for comfort, seeing ever more of the man.

As well as this affection, James's health both of body and mind concerned Marie greatly. He complained much of pains, and sought the help of physicians and even an astrologer. It all made an anxious time for her, pregnant again as she was, whatever else, her husband not lacking in ability in bed.

For the realm, also, it was a testing period, King Henry sending envoys to demand that James came to meet him at York, this to agree to enforce a putting down of the Roman Catholic Church in Scotland, as he had done in England. Although not particularly religiously minded, and believing that anyway his Creator was condemning him to hell, James did not have any reforming zeal. Cardinal Beaton, ever having greater say in the rule of the nation, strongly urged refusal to meet the Tudor. Henry, angry, declared that if James would not come to meet him, *he* would come to Scotland, and in armed strength.

It looked as though war might add to James's other troubles, that autumn of 1541, with Beaton offering to help finance conflict with England, if necessary, out of the great wealth of Holy Church.

Marie had a sufficiency of problems the following summer and autumn of 1542. Why had she ever agreed to wed James of Scotland?

Henry Tudor was making no idle threat. He began to

assemble an army to march north. And at word of it James, despite having no lack of experienced commanders among his lords, of all men chose his peculiar friend Oliver Sinclair to lead a Scots force to defend the realm, to the disquiet of the said magnates, he deeming himself too unwell to command in person.

In the circumstances, it was no great force that mustered, once the harvest was in, the lords distancing themselves, in fact most of the men coming from Church lands, at Beaton's expense.

Reports indicated that the English army was gathering at Carlisle, under the Duke of Norfolk, an able commander. So Sinclair was sent down to the West March with the force, and with instructions to collect mosstroopers from the lords and lairds of the Debateable Land, the Maxwells, Johnstones, Armstrongs and the rest. Unfortunately, these scornfully refused to serve under so inexperienced and little-esteemed a commander as Sinclair, making the Scots array as modest in numbers as it was poorly led.

Lacking much in the way of cavalry, such supporters as Sinclair had managed to collect advised that soft ground, marshland, would be the best on which to confront the enemy, who would almost certainly be strong in mounted troops, the horses' hooves apt to sink into the bogland and so be greatly hindered. Therefore the area at the head of the Solway Firth was chosen, where the Rivers Esk and Liddel and Lyne flowed but sluggishly towards salt water, and there was much marsh, the Solway Moss.

There, a distinctly insufficient and inexpertly led Scots army placed itself, to await the onslaught of Norfolk's veteran host.

The inevitable happened. The English attacked on three

fronts, seeking to make the watery land fight for them, with their own Marchmen guiding, outnumbering and outmanoeuvring the Scots, whose morale was low anyway, and with no faith in their leader. They made but a poor defence. And when, seeing probable defeat looming, Oliver Sinclair quite openly fled the field, the day was lost, and most feebly. The defenders followed the lead of their commander and likewise abandoned the fight. It was one of the most shameful episodes in Scots military history.

The English did not advance far into Scotland, for the mosstrooping Marchmen, however unwilling they had been to support Sinclair, were strong in their opposition to any invasion of *their* territory, and were well able to exploit the defensive nature of the Debateable Land highly effectively. Norfolk had no orders for any major conquest attempt on Scotland and, satisfied, turned back for Carlisle.

Marie was at her dower-palace of Linlithgow awaiting childbirth again, James with her hoping for another son to be his successor, depressed, unwell and continually declaring that the finger of God was upon him, however much his wife sought to hearten him, she herself mourning her two small sons.

When the news of Solway Moss reached them, the king collapsed entirely. But it was not so much the defeat of his army that seemed to shake him, as the state of his friend Sinclair.

"Oliver fled! Is Oliver taken? Oh, Oliver fled! Where? Here is God's curse on me! Where is my Oliver?" This was his reaction.

Marie told him that it need not be disaster. The English had turned back. Sinclair had escaped, and there having been but little of battle, no great loss of life had been occasioned. But James was not to be consoled. He was a doomed man, and deservedly, he asserted. He had failed the nation as monarch.

He was still more concerned over Sinclair than with aught else, including his wife's condition. Oliver would certainly not make for Linlithgow, the queen's palace. He would go to Falkland where he would expect to find his curious friend.

However near to childbirth Marie was, James left her there and made for Queen Margaret's Ferry, to ride to Falkland.

Marie never saw her husband alive again, remaining at Linlithgow for the birth. On the Day of the Conception of the Blessed Virgin Mary, 8 December, her child was born, a girl this time, whom she decided to name Mary, not after herself but because of the day.

James, she judged, would be further dejected that she had not produced another son to heir his throne. But at least the infant appeared to be healthy, and sucked strongly at her breasts.

It was weeks later before she heard the sad tidings from one of James's attendants. At Falkland, still awaiting the arrival of the missing Sinclair, and a very sick man, learning that he now had a daughter, he had exclaimed, with groans, that "it came with a lass and it will gang with a lass!" He meant that the crown had come to the Stewarts through the marriage of Bruce's daughter Marjory to Walter the High Steward; and now there was only this female infant to succeed him. He had taken to his bed, refused food, turned his face to the wall, and positively sought death – and shortly he had found it.

Scotland had a queen-regent for a queen-regnant for the first time, unless the child Maid of Norway, Margaret, who died at Orkney at the end of the thirteenth century could be so termed, granddaughter of Alexander the Third. Now the diminutive Mary was Queen of Scots. And that meant, in effect, with no close male kinsman to act as regent, Marie de Guise, a Frenchwoman, was now governor of Scotland. How would the Scots take that?

Marie herself, grateful for the new and healthy daughter, but still grieving sorely for the two sons who had died, faced the prospect questioningly.

5

The Scots did not. The notion of a woman ruling the land did not appeal to either the nobles or the churchmen, and a foreign woman at that, however valuable was the Auld Alliance with France in keeping the English at bay. Arran proposed betrothal of his young son to the infant queen. He was the nearest male heir to the crown, a grandson of James the Third, his mother the Princess Mary having married the second Lord Hamilton who was then created Earl of Arran. Although a weak man in most matters, he was a strong believer that Holy Church should be reformed from many of its degeneracies, and large numbers of so-called Protestants rallied behind his name. Henry Tudor, who had cast adrift from Rome, backed him in this, no doubt hoping to use him in his desire to wed Edward, Prince of Wales to the new little queen and thereby gain control of Scotland. So Cardinal Beaton and the Catholics were strongly opposed, and founded another party in Scotland which Marie, reared in a religious family, was all but forced to back. In the circumstances, a distinctly precarious situation.

Marie sought to steer a middle course, none so easy, especially when the Earl of Lennox, ever at odds with Arran, married the Lady Margaret Douglas, daughter of Angus and Margaret Tudor and so a niece of King Henry, this pushing him more or less into the English camp and producing a third faction in Scotland.

Beaton was anxious to emphasise the Auld Alliance with France. Fortunately Arran was not against this, so a parliament in December was able by a clear majority to renew the French connection. Lennox hit back by promising to do all he could to arrange a betrothal between the infant Queen Mary and Edward, Prince of Wales, with Henry agreeing that if this was satisfactorily concluded he would see that Lennox was made Governor of Scotland under his own lord-paramountcy.

The Tudor did more than make promises. He declared war, not on Scotland as such but on the forces of Beaton and Arran – which was, in effect, on Marie, this in April of 1544, challenging by land and sea. Lord Lisle, England's High Admiral, with no fewer than two hundred ships, was sent north with the Earl of Hertford and ten thousand men to land at Leith and march on Edinburgh.

The capital city had a notably strong and effective provost, Sir Adam Otterburn of Reidhall. He hastily mustered the citizenry to arms, and sent word to Marie at Linlithgow to flee to the safety of Stirling Castle. In person, he rode to Leith under a white flag of truce, to demand what Hertford meant by landing with armed men on Scottish soil when the two nations were not at war. Hertford answered that he had not come to parley but to do battle. Otterburn declared that the people of Edinburgh would defend their city to the last man, to Hertford's hooted laughter. Let them try so to do, he declared.

It was, to be sure, a hopeless defence, the townsmen, however stout in their efforts, no match for the English knights, spearmen, archers and cannoneers. Because the foe, coming by sea, had no cavalry, Otterburn and some of the wealthier citizens, mounted, did achieve some success, but this represented only a delaying of disaster.

Soon the defenders were vanquished and dying in their hundreds, and only the fortress on its rock-top held out, its artillery superior to that brought up from the ships. The city itself was put to the torch, the townsfolk fleeing with such belongings as they might carry, this to the heights of Arthur's Seat and the Blackford and Braid Hills and the open country beyond. Soon all the capital was ablaze, under a pall of smoke which hung above it for days, glowing red at night.

Beaton, Arran, Argyll and the other lords and clerics joined Marie and the little queen at Linlithgow. They urged her to take the child to Stirling Castle, which she had not yet done, it all but impregnable, while they moved still further north to Perth, there at the gateway to the Highlands, to seek to gather strength from the clan chiefs, whose fighting abilities were renowned.

Informed of this last, Hertford and Lisle contented themselves with ravaging and laying waste all the adjacent towns and countryside, with unparalleled ferocity, this on the direct orders of their monarch. But the Highlanders' threat from Perth was sufficient to cause pro-English Angus and his Douglases, immured in his Tantallon Castle, to switch allegiance once again; and Hertford decided that enough was enough meantime. He and Lisle set fire to the port of Leith, to match the still-smouldering Edinburgh, and sailed off southwards.

For the time being, Scotland was left to its own internal feudings and faction fightings. None doubted, however, that Henry Tudor's determination to gain the northern kingdom by the marriage of his son to the infant queen, which was becoming known as the Rough Wooing, would continue.

On the third day of June, at Stirling, Marie, in the

queen's name, ordered the feeble Arran to call not a parliament but a great meeting of the lords, barons, chiefs and magnates, to unite in preserving, or rather restoring, the independence of the realm. And this great gathering, recognising the all too evident weakness of Arran as legislator and leader, and the very different strength of mind of the Frenchwoman, appointed *her* to be regent of Scotland for her little daughter, now in her eighteenth month, with full powers to rule the realm.

Marie de Guise had become the lawful and accepted governor of her adopted country.

Henry Tudor, ever the menace, was Marie's main preoccupation. How to circumvent him? Somehow Scotland's warring factions must be united, if at all possible. A coalition? Beaton's Catholics, Arran's Protestants, Angus's pro-English party, the feuding Highland chiefs and equally feuding Borderers, the Kennedys, "kings of Carrick" and their Ayrshire and Galloway opponents?

Oddly, it was Henry himself who helped in this. For he sent Sir Ralph Eure north to harry the Borderland that July of 1544, with thousands of men; and Eure in his savage enthusiasm, among other depredations and destructions, part-demolished Melrose Abbey. This was the Douglas burial-place, where Angus's ancestors were interred. In fury Angus swore vengeance.

Marie saw her opportunity. However little she admired and trusted the Douglas, she had him created Lieutenant-General of the Realm, with the royal authority to muster as large an army as he could to deal with Eure and his colleagues. This he was not slow in doing. Assembling a large force of his own Douglases, the Homes, Kerrs and other Borderers, he met Eure and Bowes and Layton on

Ancrum Moor, just south of the Eildon Hills and St Boswells, none so far from Melrose itself. So hot were the Borders folk against the Eure devastations that large numbers of the local population joined Angus's force as camp-followers. And one young woman distinguished herself by fighting most valorously, so much so that when an English battleaxe severed both her feet from her legs, she fought on until loss of blood felled her unconscious. Her name was Lilliard, and her exploit became so renowned that the hillock where her part of the battle took place, on Ancrum Moor, became known as Lilliard's Edge. And the rhyme was devised:

Fair Maiden Lilliard lies under this stane,
　Little was her stature but great was her fame;
Upon the English loons she laid many thumps,
　And when her legs were cuttied off she fought
　　　　upon her stumps.

Eure, defeated, returned to Carlisle.

So Marie had the victorious Angus, who had headed the pro-English faction, now on her side against Henry, and even associating with Beaton.

The cardinal had his own plans and designs. This aim of the Tudor, to have the child Queen of Scots marry his son Edward, could, he declared, be circumvented by marrying her off to the son and heir of the King of France, the dauphin, thus further strengthening the Auld Alliance against England. Marie, after two less than successful marriages in the cause of national expediency, was doubtful about this, hoping that her small daughter might one day be in a position to choose a husband for herself. She withheld agreement, this at Yuletide of 1545.

Then, in the March, following, there was a great

upheaval. Arran's Protestant cause was becoming ever more assertive, however poor he was at playing the leader, many of the clergy themselves supporting it, especially as they saw the sons, legal or otherwise, of lords being promoted to bishoprics and abbacies in return for lands gifted to the Church. One of these objecting priests, by the name of George Wishart, was vocal enough to have the cardinal decide not only that he be silenced but be made an example of. He had him burned at the stake at St Andrews on a charge of heresy, he and his mistress, Marion Ogilvie, watching the proceedings from his palatial St Andrews Castle. The Protestant faction rose in wrath, and a group led by Norman Leslie, Master of Rothes, who had actually been a friend of Beaton's, through that friendship gained access to the strongly guarded castle, and had the cardinal stabbed to death, before hanging the naked body out of the bedchamber window, swinging bloodily on a bed-sheet, this as a sign that reform in Holy Church was necessary.

Hostilities throughout the land resulted inevitably; violent civil war.

Marie was desperately worried. She had had no love for David Beaton, but she was a firm Catholic. And, of course, Henry Tudor, the Protestant monarch, saw his chance to exploit the situation, and announced strong support for the uprising, it all aiding his cause. And Angus, Scotland's Lieutenant-General, although not very religiously inclined, was Protestant.

What was Marie, the regent, to do? The nation was utterly divided. The Vatican would expect her to lead against the Protestants. But her information was that the majority of the Scots people were that way inclined. She decided that she must not seem to take sides. Her daughter, the queen, must be above factions and parties. She herself could only await events, however feeble that might seem.

In matters of religious reforms, she was much influenced by a prominent courtier, Sir David Lindsay of the Mount, Lord Lyon King of Arms, a poet and playwright. He had been a personal friend of King James, and Marie much admired his talents and wit. He was the son of another Sir David, of Garleton, in Haddingtonshire, of the line of the Lords Lindsay of the Byres. The clerics would have had him dismissed, indeed some said burned at the stake for heresy, like Wishart, but Marie maintained her friendship with him, which commended her to the reformers but not to the clerics. He served her well. There were whispers that she found him sufficiently to her taste to favour him more personally, and as Lord Lyon King of Arms and Royal Usher he had access to her person at most times. Marie was not averse to personable men's company, and there was talk, especially when, having come round to the idea, she sent him, along with Archbishop Beaton of Glasgow, nephew to the late cardinal, to France, to negotiate a treaty and confirm the betrothal of the little Queen Mary to Henry of France's son and heir. Lindsay was famed for his many sayings, a favourite being the occasion when he suggested to King James that he be made Master Tailor to the King. James, astonished, asked why, since he, Lindsay, could neither shape nor sew; to which he gave the reply, "Your Grace has approved and appointed to bishoprics and benefices many who could neither preach nor teach, so why not this?" a comment which did not commend him to the clerics. But it amused Marie.

They remained close, which further displeased the churchmen. And on this visit to France she had a personal task for him.

"David, when you have seen King Henry, will you go on to Hainault, where I have Guise lands, indeed from whence comes much of my monies. Of late, there have been delays in sending me these, I know not why. It would be kind if you would see the Lady Fleming there. She is a bastard daughter of James the Fourth, and is lady-in-waiting to my child Mary. Discover what is amiss. It is much to ask of you, but it would be a notable act of friendship."

"Your grace honours me with your benevolence. I will so do if you will give me full instructions. And this of the French prince, the dauphin? Is it to be an extension of the betrothal? Or more than that? Arrangements as to the marriage? The archbishop will know, but . . ."

"King Henry is urgent. He fears that the other Henry, the Tudor, may try to grasp my daughter by force. Send a host north to take her. So he seeks to have her wed before the Tudor could undertake such. A treaty to confirm the alliance of Scotland and France, and this marriage in token, you and the archbishop as witnesses."

"How soon? The marriage?"

"Mary is now in her fifth year. Such royal marriages can be at an early age. I seek no great delay." Marie paused. "When you visit Hainault, I have another kindness to ask of you, David. I have my son, the Duke of Longueville, now of nine years. He is in the care of my kinsfolk. Would that I could have him here with me. But that is not considered wise by my brothers, especially the Cardinal Charles. All must be done according to what is best for the Guise line! I have not a few brothers! The Duke of Aumale acts guardian for young Francis. If you could see the boy, convey my love and caring, that would please me much."

"It is little enough to do. For one I so greatly esteem."

"You are kind!" She clasped him to her, he none so

passive in that embrace. It was by no means the first time that these two had demonstrated affection. "And when you return, I desire you to contrive a pageant for me. A great celebration of the fellow-feeling between Scotland and France, the Entente Cordiale. If and when Mary is indeed wed to the dauphin, one day *he* will be King of France. And she queen of both realms, a most notable circumstance. You, so able a playwright and marker of occasions, must do this for me. And for Mary. Will you?"

"I will do a deal more than that for you, Marie, to be sure," he declared. "I would claim you as my friend and ally, as well as my liege-lady. May I?"

"You may. I am much blessed in my usher, I think!" she murmured, before he closed her lips.

6

In due course David Lindsay brought back satisfactory tidings from France, and none more so for Marie than word of her son, the Duke Francis. He was in good health and spirits. His mother was told by the master-storyteller how the boy had sent a somewhat incoherent but eloquent message. "'I wear my green suit on Sundays,'" he reported. "'My poor donkey, John, has died. Tell Madame the Queen that I have a sore head and hand. But I can hold the reins to hunt the stag. My silly dog barks – wow, wow, wow! I have a pony but I would have a big horse, a black horse. Can I have one?'"

But however happy about this amusing account, Marie was much worried over her other offspring, Mary, this on account of Henry Tudor. Although a sick man now – quite possibly on account of his persistent womanising – he was still demanding that his son Edward was to wed the young Queen Mary, and that he would ensure this, by armed force if necessary. His envoy, Sir Ralph Sadler, was ever at Marie on the subject. He would send up a host to collect her.

Perceiving this as no idle threat, Marie came to the conclusion that there was nothing for it but to send the child to France for her safety. She would install the girl in some secure hiding-place until she could be transported to Paris.

Where? Henry no doubt had his spies at the Scots court,

who would inform Sadler. Marie, once, on a visit to the Stewart country of Lennox, had been taken to see a hidden sanctuary, a small Augustinian priory, on an islet in a little-known lake, the Loch of Menteith. There were two other islets, on one a minor castle of the earldom, and the other, the Isle of Dogs, where the hunting-hounds were kept. Surely this remote hide-away would serve. She would have David Lindsay take Mary and her four little friends, all named Mary, thither, until a ship could collect them at Dumbarton and transport them to France. The reliable Lady Livingstone could look after them there.

This arranged, Marie felt less anxious, at least in this respect.

There was, however, a sufficiency of other worries. The Protestant cause was in the ascendant, and had Arran as a figurehead, however vague a character. Marie was prepared to let the religious controversy take its own course. The Scots must choose their own preferred creed. But the Catholic lords thought otherwise, and under the Gordon Earl of Huntly were seeking confrontation – and, unfortunately, expecting the queen mother actively to support them. No doubt the Vatican did also, probably the King of France likewise. But she saw it as no part of her responsibility towards her daughter's subjects. Let them decide for themselves.

And there was a very definite and vehement voice being raised on this issue, however moderate that of its high-born advocate, Arran, next heir to the throne. This, oddly, was that of no nobleman nor magnate. The son of a tenant farmer near Haddington, in Lothian, had quite suddenly surged into prominence in the Protestant cause. This young man, John Knox, a priest, had come out loudly in condemnation of Church degeneracy, and everywhere the common folk were flocking to his banner. A fiery and eloquent preacher, he was demanding reform, and drastic reform at that. He had been a disciple of George Wishart, taken up his abode at St Andrews, the ecclesiastical capital of the realm, and had been involved in the assassination of Cardinal Beaton whom he called the favourite son of Satan. Captured, he had been sent to be a galley-slave in France. Now he was back, and stirring up action.

The dramatic word reached Scotland just after Yuletide that Henry Tudor had died. None would mourn him in Scotland, even the Protestant faction. But there were fears that, even so, the consequences could be serious for the northern kingdom. For his son, nine-year-old Edward, he whom his father had wanted to marry to Queen Mary, had an ambitious and determined uncle. His mother had been Jane Seymour, Henry's third wife. Now her brother, Edward Seymour, Earl of Hertford, finding himself in a very powerful position, had his nephew create him Duke of Somerset and regent of England. A vigorous character, he decided to carry on where his Tudor brother-in-law had had to leave off. And that meant, among other matters, marrying his nephew to Mary Queen of Scots, betrothed as she was to France's dauphin, and so unite the kingdoms, ever the ambition of English rulers. And, being the man he was, it was unlikely that he would delay action.

Would the Scots put aside their religious bickering meantime to confront this almost certain menace? Marie prayed that they would. She sought David Lindsay's aid to get little Mary off to France.

So she and Lindsay had Sir Andrew Wood hasten to take a ship round the mass of Scotland from Fife to Dumbarton. They would bring the child to him there. It was the Loch of Menteith for them, and the little island priory.

Lady Livingstone was with the children, the five Marys, the other four the daughters of the Lords Seton, Fleming, Livingstone and Beaton of Balfour. They would all go to France, Lady Livingstone with them.

From Stirling it was some twenty miles up the infant Forth to their loch, where, on the shore, a great bell hung which, beaten, sent its summons echoing from the surrounding hillsides, and in due course brought the monks rowing their boat to collect the visitors. The horses had to be left at a nearby stable.

How good it was for Marie to see her daughter with her little friends, although at the back of her mind was the thought that she would be taking her off for a further and possibly lengthy parting. But that was life. If only she could have gone back to France, her own homeland, with her child, to rejoin her young Francis and her brothers and settle there for a normal family life. But that was not for her, mother and representative of the Queen of Scots, with her late husband's kingdom to help to rule. David Lindsay was a comfort, however.

Arranging for the girls to depart their island sanctuary, with all their gear, amid much childish excitement, took time, and that night was spent at the little priory, the monks kind hosts, although keeping the men well apart from the women overnight. In the morning it was the Clyde and Dumbarton for them.

They rode through very lovely scenery of what was called the Trossachs westwards of Aberfoyle, past Lochs Katrine and Arklet, and then down long Loch Lomondside, under the towering mountain of that name to the lochfoot at Balloch, and on through the seven miles of the Vale of Leven to the Clyde at Dumbarton, all Lennox or Levenach Stewart country. At the royal castle there, on its rock, they heard the news. Somerset had invaded Scotland, with the Earl of Southampton, advancing from Berwick through the Merse, and sending his artillery by sea to be landed at Leith, with more men, this in no fewer than thirty-four ships and thirty transports, commanded by the admiral, Lord Clinton. Somerset had halted at Salt Preston, to which Clinton moved from Leith with the cannon; and the next day they met the Scots, under Arran, Angus, Argyll, Huntly and other lords, at Pinkie near Musselburgh. The Scots suffered a dire defeat, with fourteen thousand slain.

Gravely concerned, needless to say, Marie clearly had to return to Stirling as speedily as possible, and seek to rally the Highlands and the north-east in order to keep Somerset and Clinton from advancing further. She much doubted whether Arran would act with any efficacy. So it was a hasty goodbye to little Mary and her friends, with Lady Livingstone. Admiral Wood would take them to France, while she, with Lindsay and Lennox and other lords whom they could pick up, rode eastwards, anxious indeed.

At Perth they found the northern Scots lords, under Argyll and Huntly and the Highland chiefs of Mackintosh, Macpherson and Cameron, waiting for the western clansmen to arrive, the MacDonalds, MacLeods, Macleans and MacIans. Stirling was the traditional location at which to seek to hold up any enemy advance from the south, with the Forth estuary stretching eastwards, and the marshy levels of the Flanders Moss lying to the west all but impassable for cavalry. Here was the so strategic bridge.

Marie was thankful to find Argyll really in command, although Arran was present, for he was an able fighter. Unfortunately his Campbells and many of the other clans were perpetually at feud, especially with the MacDonalds, which tended to limit Argyll's usefulness. But the presence of the queen mother had a unifying influence. Marie recognised that, however unsuitable for a woman to march with an armed host, she must so do, at least at this stage.

When the West Highlanders and Islesmen arrived, there was debate as to whether they should march south to confront Somerset, or wait at the strong defensive site at Stirling, where so many battles had been won and lost. Arran, as could have been anticipated, recommended waiting, Marie urging, with Argyll and Huntly and the chiefs, advance.

The word was that Somerset, having taken and sacked Edinburgh – although not its all but impregnable citadel – was at Leith and Musselburgh embarking his troops on Clinton's large fleet. Whither was he bound in these? No doubt he knew well of the problems of seeking victory at Stirling. Was he just aiming to cross Forth to Fife and march west from there? Or go on to the Tay with his army to get behind the Scots in the Perth area? Until they knew the answer to this it was hard to decide on the best strategy. They awaited information anxiously.

When sure word came, it was unexpectedly encouraging. Somerset had suddenly turned and gone back south. Apparently there had developed an extraordinary situation in which his own brother, the Lord Seymour, with whom he did not get on, had more or less captured the young King Edward and was making a bid for supreme power in England, this aided by Dudley, Earl of Warwick. Somerset admittedly had left Clinton and his ships, with most of the armed host, still in Scotland; but in these circumstances it seemed unlikely that there would be any major onslaught in his absence. But he would be back, almost certainly. So it seemed to be a matter of waiting.

Then they learned that the Borders barons, the Homes in especial, had not been content to wait. Angry at their Merse being invaded, they had rallied their neighbours, the Kerrs and Elliots, the Turnbulls and Scotts, the Armstrongs and Johnstones and the rest, and were attacking the rear of the English host.

That was enough for Argyll, Huntly and the clan chiefs. They were not to be beaten by the Borderers. Advance then, Marie encouraging them. They moved on, heading for Edinburgh, devastated as it was.

Marie went with them as far as Linlithgow, her dower-palace, where, at David Lindsay's urging, she left them. If there was to be fighting, a woman's presence was no advantage and could be dangerous to her. She was too precious to hazard herself.

It was two days later that David brought her the tidings. Clinton, presumably on instructions from Somerset, had embarked the English host on his fleet at Leith and sailed off southwards, his support seemingly required elsewhere.

One more threat to Scotland was removed, meantime at any rate.

They heard the reason behind this development in due course: led by that brother of Somerset's, the Lord Seymour, there had been all but a palace revolution. Warwick used him in his attempts to bring down the Protector of the Throne, as Somerset was now styling himself. Seymour was taken and confined in the Tower of London. The House of Lords, at his brother's urging, passed a sentence of high treason on him. He was duly beheaded on Tower Hill without delay: so much for sibling relations.

Warwick mustered his considerable forces in the West Country and Norfolk, these amounting to no fewer than twenty thousand armed men, led by supporting lords and knights. He was a noted warrior who had distinguished himself at the Battle of Pinkie. Somerset sought to play down this opposition by offering his daughter's hand in marriage to Warwick's son, but this gesture was not accepted. Then Somerset carried off the young king to Windsor Castle, from Whitehall, and shut himself up there, calling on the nobles to rise in his favour, this to no great effect. Warwick had the power in men, and used it. Windsor was taken, the young monarch held, and Somerset with him. Lord Protector he might be, but his protecting was of no avail. He was taken to the Tower, condemned for high treason, like his late brother, and hanged at Tower Hill. So ended the rule of one of the most powerful men England had known for long.

Sighs of relief were drawn all over Scotland at least, Marie's among them. But would Warwick prove any less aggressive?

7

Marie received an invitation to attend the wedding of one of her brothers, the Duke of Aumale, to Princess Anne, daughter of King Henry of France; but with the quarrelling between the Catholic and Protestant lords dividing Scotland, and until she was fairly sure that Warwick would not imitate his predecessor to endeavour to grasp the northern kingdom, she felt that she could not leave her adopted country, having no faith in Arran's ability to conduct its affairs.

She received frequent letters from the Ladies Livingstone and Fleming at Paris regarding her daughter. All seemed to be well with Mary, her two chaperones reported. The gossip that reached her otherwise from France was that Lady Fleming – Joanna, an illegitimate daughter of James the Fourth by the Countess of Bothwell – was demonstrating her royal connections by becoming the mistress of King Henry there, which was arousing the wrath of Queen Catherine de Medici, who was no gentle woman to offend. As a result, Lady Fleming had to leave France, even though she had borne the king a son, Henry of Valois, known as the Bastard of Angoulême. So another chaperone had to be appointed to partner Lady Livingstone, one Madame Parois. But at least the cheerful extrovert Joanna Fleming came home to inform Marie of all Mary's circumstances at the French court.

It was hoped that conditions in Scotland would allow her to visit France before long.

This Catholic–Protestant conflict was a great worry to Marie – not so much in the religious context as in her efforts to keep the peace of the realm. For her two most able and powerful commanders, the Earls of Huntly and Argyll, were on opposite sides, Huntly a fervent Catholic, Argyll converted to Protestantism. They did not actually come to blows, but there was friction between them. David Lindsay, who was Marie's competent envoy to the two earls, as to others, ferrying between them and seeking to keep them from taking active leads in the conflict of the faith, did his best. But with John Knox and his like ever more vehement in their advocacy of violent reform, it was all like a powder-keg waiting to explode. Marie's Catholic upbringing was known to all, and however much she sought to present a neutral image in the struggle, the assumption was that she was anti-Protestant, and that her daughter, the queen, would be also. Knox thundered against Scotland's crown being in the hands of the like, this causing Huntly to claim that the divine ought to be arrested on a charge of treason.

David Lindsay was a great comfort to Marie in all this, as in so much else. As Royal Usher and Lord Lyon King of Arms, his association with her could not be criticised; but the whisperings were ever there and discretion called for. Who would be the mother of a child queen in a foreign country?

One unlooked-for development had its compensations in this respect: trouble in the Isles, not religious trouble, for zealous reform had not reached that far, but feuding on a larger scale than usual, which spilled over, this on account of the MacDonald–Campbell traditional hostility, rather different from the normal clan feuding. John MacDonald of Moidart, Chief of Clanranald, was as unruly as he was powerful among the clans, and now he overreached all acceptance by raiding and abducting women and stealing cattle much further south than his normal, not exactly into Campbell country but none so far off, across great Loch Linnhe and into the Ballachulish, Loch Etive and Glencoe areas, which Argyll was apt to see as within his sphere of influence. The Campbell demanded redress, Arran showed no interest, and Marie, anxious that full-scale Highland warfare should not break out between these two largest clans and their allies, felt that she had to step in. Careful not to summon him to Campbell territory, she ordered Clanranald to appear before her and Arran at Inverness, as a neutral location, having more or less to coerce the so-called governor to attend, he grumbling at her demands. And he complained the more when the MacDonald contemptuously refused to appear before them, declaring that no one was going to order *him* into their presence in his own Highlands, especially a woman and a Stewart.

Marie saw this defiance as dangerous indeed, whatever Arran felt. She was acting as the Queen of Scots' representative, and if she let the MacDonald get away with this, who knew how far such scornful repudiation might spread among the clans. Clanranald must be shown that the royal authority prevailed, even in the far Western Highlands and Isles.

There was nothing for it but an expedition and show of strength. And to display this in those faraway and difficult parts warships and cannon would be necessary.

Sir Andrew Wood of Largo, the admiral, was now a very old man. But his son, another Andrew, had more or less succeeded him, acting the admiral. Marie ordered him to come over to Leith with some of his vessels, to make the required demonstration.

Wood duly arrived with no fewer than six warships equipped with the desired artillery, all these and the crews paid for, it was often recounted, mainly out of old Sir Andrew's renowned source of wealth, walrus-tusk ivory from Iceland, which only such as he, with the necessary ships, could obtain, and apparently much in demand by the Hansa merchants of the Baltic.

David Lindsay, needless to say, accompanied Marie on this challenging occasion. Before they sailed, she thought it suitable that Wood should be promoted to the rank of knight, like his father. She could appoint to knighthood; but a knight could only be actually made by another knight. And a woman could not be a knight, however royal and important. So she had David dub Wood, there on his ship, she with her hand also on the sword-hilt, naming him *Sir* Andrew, to the cheers of his crewmen, a worthy start for their expedition.

Despite the intention of intimidating Clanranald, a sort of holiday atmosphere prevailed. Fortunately the weather was kind and the seas fairly calm as they sailed north up the coasts of Fife, Angus, Aberdeenshire and Moray, and across that great firth, and on up the Ross, Sutherland and Caithness shoreline, Marie greatly looking forward to another visit to the Isles, which she had so much enjoyed on that earlier occasion. It was only when they turned westwards into the Pentland Firth, where the tides of the Atlantic competed with the swirls and currents created by the Orkney Isles, these known as roosts, that the ships began to toss and heave, to Marie's discomfort. She was not actually sick, but affected enough not to feel desirous of eating. David assured her that once they rounded Cape

Wrath, the extreme north-west tip of mainland Scotland, there would be less heaving and plunging, to be succeeded by sidelong rolling, probably less upsetting, this until they were among the more sheltered waters of the Hebridean isles.

He was proved accurate, and soon Marie was able to forget a queasy stomach in her renewed wonder and admiration of the scenery, the drama and colour of it all, a delight to the eye. The hundreds, all but thousands of islands, great and small, with their cliffs and corries, seal-dotted skerries and reefs, castle-crowned headlands and deer-populated slopes, again captivated her regard in ongoing succession, David able to point out and name most of the prominent items, and the clans and chieftains who owned them, his heraldic authority as Lyon King of Arms making him particularly knowledgeable on such matters.

The six ships would not go unnoticed in these waters. Marie wondered whether Clanranald would be warned of their coming. They saw many of the longships and galleys used by the Islesmen, singly and in groups, and one or more of these greyhounds of the seas, as they were called, could push on to inform the MacDonald, faster with their long, ranked oars than any vessels dependent on sails and variable winds. But, proud as he was, Clanranald would be unlikely to make himself scarce in this his own country.

Moidart, a large mainland peninsula, lay, or rather thrust itself out into the Sea of the Hebrides fully one hundred and eighty miles south of Cape Wrath. Its chief's principal seat was the famous Castle Tioram, renowned as being one of the largest and strongest fortalices in the Isles, set on a tidal islet in the mouth of Loch Moidart, this just north of the great Ardnamurchan headland, the most westerly point of all mainland Scotland. Reaching this, although it was nearly full tide, they could not get the ships close, owing to the shallow depth of the water.

Sending men in small boats to assail it would be asking for trouble, for Clanranald's own galleys, much less deep of keel, would be able to attack and destroy them, undoubtedly. Wood declared that cannon-fire was the only answer; but Marie was reluctant to bombard the castle even if they could get the warships within range. A cannonade of blank shot? That might serve as a threat, with Clanranald probably not aware of the fact that effective fire was not more than three hundred yards, at least against masonry.

So it was noise and threat, created on a major scale, rather than any real efforts at damage, for Wood was concerned not to send any actual ball at the walls since their ineffectiveness would be obvious. A great cannonade of blank shot was therefore fired from all the ships; and admittedly the effect, magnified by the echoes from the surrounding hills, made a fearsome din; and however great the waste of gunpowder there was no doubt as to the dramatic challenge and the hoped-for impact.

In fact, after no great expenditure of the token aggression, results were produced. Two sheets were hung, to flap from the battlements of Castle Tioram, not exactly white flags but clearly a gesture of submission. The MacDonald was not going to risk further defiance. Then half a dozen longships and birlinns rowed out into the shallow waters, into which the larger ships dared not venture, scattering this way and that, presumably Clanranald on one of them.

There seemed to be nothing more that could usefully be done. The MacDonald had not actually capitulated, but fled the scene. His castle was all but impregnable on its islet. It could be besieged and its people eventually starved out. But to what advantage, if its owner was gone? He almost certainly had other strongholds in his domains, some which their ships could not get near.

Marie said that it was enough, Lindsay agreeing with her. Clanranald had demonstrated his inability to outface the royal authority, even in his own Moidart. Let that serve, meantime at any rate. And let all the Islesmen take note.

8

The sudden death of young King Edward the Sixth of England, however sad, was initially of advantage to Scotland, for his elder sister Mary became queen, and she was a strong-minded woman, a resolute Catholic and desirous of good relations with France, and therefore with Scotland. Sadler, now *her* envoy, was not long in reflecting these feelings. Marie, anxious to encourage this improved state of affairs, came to the conclusion that her goodwill could be proved by personally seeking to better that traditional and unending bickering and feuding on the West March of the Borderland. She would go there, taking Argyll and Huntly to emphasise her authority, picking up Scott of Buccleuch, the Lord Home and Kerr of Ferniehirst on the way. This ought to impress the English Warden and his unruly fellow-countrymen and mosstroopers – and indeed their own Scots ones – and help improve relations over this ever most troublesome area in Scots-English relations.

It made a notable occasion, for it was a long time since a Scottish monarch had made a peaceful visit to these parts, and would help to heal the repercussions of the Solway Moss disaster. Marie was not actually monarch, of course, but reigned in the name of her little daughter. So much display was demonstrated, quite a major force of earls, lords, knights and lairds accompanying her, the affair developing into a sort of benevolent progress instead of any threatening display of governmental strength. To emphasise the goodwill behind it all and the amity between Scotland, England and now France, she rode across the Solway marshes to visit Carlisle, taking D'Oysel, the French ambassador, with her, where they were well received by the bishop thereof and the local magnates.

Unfortunately, on return to Edinburgh, it was to find that not all her daughter's subjects were in favour of Scottish, English and French concord. Some three hundred lords and knights had assembled in protest and were waiting at Holyrood, to inform the queen mother that this of seeking association with the new Queen Mary Tudor was as good as an invitation to her to come north and seek to take over Scotland, as had ever been the English monarchial aim. This Tudor would merely be seeking to do so by lulling Scots fears with seeming friendliness. The Frenchwoman regent just did not understand the underlying situation. The Leopards of England did not change their spots.

Marie shook her head over this attitude, but found it hard to dispel. Not a few of the lords urged her to go to France, there to emphasise the continuing French threat to England should there be any moves against Scotland, whatever the seeming amiability of this latest Tudor.

Marie decided that, seeming to placate these objectors, she would indeed go over to France, but not really for such reasons. She wanted to see her daughter; but as well as that to seek to have her brother Charles, Cardinal of Lorraine, go to the Vatican to persuade the Pope that no vehement measures should be ordered against the Scottish reformers, emphasising that the man Knox was not typical, and that an understanding of the need for internal reform among the senior clergy was what was required. There were great abuses prevalent, mainly concerned with the grasping of ever more Church lands, and the wealth brought therefrom; and the appointment of new bishops and abbots who were totally unworthy to be so promoted, these often the bastard sons of great lords. She was loyal and strong in her Catholic faith, but was well aware of the need for reform. Let this be allowed to take its own course, so long as the peace and wellbeing of the nation was preserved, and contrary action not seen to emanate from Rome. In this attitude she was wisely and ably guided by David Lindsay, who introduced her to a very different Sinclair from the late Oliver, her husband's friend, this Henry, Dean of Glasgow, a noted scholar and statesman, who had proved his abilities on numerous occasions.

Marie consulted with the dean, who strongly advised ongoing and very evident reform, pointing out that some of the recently appointed senior clerics could not even recite the Lord's Prayer, much less the liturgy, this an indication of reaction to the extreme measures of the late Cardinal David Beaton. She made this Dean Henry her personal chaplain, and he became influential at court, to the advantage of moderate but progressive improvement in religious observance, making Knox's fulminations of greatly less relevance.

Lindsay and the dean joined in urging the calling of a parliament, this to allow the nation's views on the matter of religious reform to be expressed and acted upon. The assembly was duly called, to meet at Edinburgh that June of 1555. The Chancellor, who would preside, perhaps unfortunately was George, Earl of Huntly, one of the most vehement Catholics in the realm; but this was counterbalanced by Archibald, Earl of Argyll being not only Vice-Chancellor but High Justiciar, which made these two strong men equal in power, in parliament as in armed strength and influence. The last thing sought was a confrontation and war of words, yet that seemed to be all inescapable. Marie, who would occupy the throne in the name of her daughter, and therefore have some direction of the conduct of affairs, was determined that the will of the people, not just that of the most powerful lords and clerics, should prevail, a responsibility indeed.

When Lindsay as Lord Lyon, with his heralds, to trumpeting, had brought in the earls, as representing the ancient *ri* or lesser kings of the Celtic regime, and the bishops and mitred abbots as Royal Usher, he called on all to stand for the entry of the queen mother. Marie, after seating herself, quite promptly rose again, signing for all to sit, but herself still standing, and made her announcement.

"My lords spiritual and temporal, commissioners for the shires and royal burghs, and other representatives of the nation, I greet you warmly. This day we have to decide on the best interests of this realm in all matters in dispute, in especial religious dispute, difficult as this may be, indeed must be. I crave and pray for your good and fair judgment in this, as in all else. This ancient nation is eager for reform where error has crept in, and this must be established. It will not be easy, I repeat, without seeming to harm the interests of some who have been prominent in the previous Church ministry, and not only for prelates and clergy." She paused, as murmurs arose throughout the assembly.

"To aid us all in this reform, I, as now regent for my royal daughter, have brought from France an able and experienced cleric, Monsieur de Rubay, who together with the Archbishop Beaton of Glasgow, Dean Sinclair and Sir David Lindsay, Lord Lyon King of Arms and Royal Usher, will act as my advisers, with full recognition of the prevailing will and needs of the people. To enable him to act with the necessary authority, I propose to appoint him to the office of keeper of the Great Seal, and assistant Vice-Chancellor to my lord Earl of Argyll. Is this agreed?"

Again there was some outcry and dispute, a French Catholic being made coadjutor to the Protestant Campbell chief; but most recognised it as a worthy step in ordering the dire challenge between the religious convictions which were in danger of tearing the nation apart.

Marie sat, to allow the controversy to take its course, with representatives of both sides jumping up and asserting their demands and preferences, Huntly having to bang his gavel frequently for some sort of order. It was all very well for radical divines like Master Knox to fulminate, curse and shake the fist; but parliament had to act with calmer and reasoned judgment.

When Marie thought that sufficient time had been given for all sides to make their attitudes known, and the Chancellor was looking exasperated and glancing towards her, she rose again, which after a few moments had the desired effect.

"I propose that a council be set up, to consider all sides of this important issue," she announced. "I understand that there has been frequently such a representative body called upon, named, I think, the Lords of the Articles, this in the past making valuable recommendations on great issues such as this. Is it agreed that such be instructed to consider it all, and make report to another session of this parliament in due course?"

Clearly that was the wish of the majority present, the very vocal wish. The Chancellor and Justiciar were so ordered to arrange it, with loud advice from the enthusiasts on both sides.

Thankfully Marie signed to Lindsay to have his trumpeters indicate the end of the session, and to usher her out from the hall.

She was not against Reformation coming to Scotland, but could have done without it having to be in *her* regency.

9

Shortly after that parliament, Marie was faced with an extraordinary situation, once more, for a Frenchwoman and a Catholic. Henry the Eighth's elder daughter Mary, now Queen of England, was the opposite of her father, a perfervid Catholic, and she had appointed Cardinal Pole, Archbishop of Canterbury, to be her chief minister. He was a harsh and violent man, who had had burned at the stake, as heretics, no fewer than two hundred and eighty Protestants, five bishops among them, including his predecessor Cranmer, Archbishop of Canterbury. A kinsman of the queen, a descendant of Henry the Seventh, he was supporting Spain in a war with France, and he had Queen Mary demanding that Scotland end its ancient alliance with France and send ships and men to join the English aid to Spain, this on threat of armed retaliation if refused.

Marie had to call for an urgent meeting of those newly appointed Lords of the Articles to make reply to this. At least the English challenge had the effect of uniting Huntly and Argyll and the other religious disputants meantime; they were not going to side with England and Spain against France. Some demonstration of this attitude seemed to be called for, which the dominant Pole would not fail to recognise.

Probably through the machinations of Cardinal Pole, Mary Tudor was wed to King Philip of Spain, this of course to the detriment of France. King Henry the Second thereof sent pleas to Scotland to make some demonstration of the Auld Alliance by an invasion of England.

Marie was reluctant to involve her daughter's realm in outright war; but on the advice of Lindsay and Dean Sinclair she urged the ever-ready Borderers to make larger and deeper assaults into Northumberland and Cumberland, from Tweed to Solway, an extension of their customary behaviour, which she could claim as some fulfilment of Henry's request. But this was judged insufficient for French purposes, being little more than normal border-raiding, especially when Lord Home, Warden of the East March, suffered a severe defeat by the opposing Percy and other Northumbrians at Blackbrae, this in November.

Something more definite and evident had to be done to threaten England and aid France. Marie ordered an army to assemble at Kelso, only a few miles from the borderline, and sent the French envoy, D'Oysel, to build up a fortified position and base at Eyemouth, near to Berwick, whose fine harbour for Wood's ships would pose a parallel gesture, she hoping that this would be sufficient to alarm the English and restrain any assault across the Channel.

To her chagrin, her most powerful lords, including Argyll and Huntly, Home and Cassillis, refused to comply, declaring that the Borderers' assaults had been sufficient to display alliance with France. If there was actually an English attack on Scotland they would demonstrate their strength; but they were not going to challenge the Auld *Enemy* unnecessarily on behalf of the Auld *Alliance* on this occasion.

Marie, disappointed and frustrated, sought to shame the earls into support by staging an attack on Wark Castle, an English stronghold just across Tweed west of Coldstream, with D'Oysel's men and some of the Borderers. This was to be only a token gesture, for it was a very powerful fortalice of the Prince-Bishops of Durham, and only a lengthy siege would be likely to starve it into submission; but a move across the river's ford here, in strength, would demonstrate that the Scots were to be reckoned with, and hopefully restrain Mary Tudor and Cardinal Pole from active assault on France, this the more necessary in that the port of Calais, long held by the English, was presently being assailed by the Guise brothers, who greatly resented this enemy toehold in France.

So Marie, with David Lindsay, personally presented herself before Wark, demanding its surrender. As expected, this was refused, and the Scots force settled down around the castle in a great encampment, Marie and Lindsay occupying side-by-side tents, to their mutual satisfaction. It was not really a genuine siege, for that would take overlong, and the gaining of the castle was not of any major importance. What was important was that the Scots should be seen to be prepared for anti-English action should France be assailed and Calais reinforced.

Whatever Wark's garrison thought of it, the besiegers saw it as a sort of holiday in the pleasant May weather, with hunting and hawking in the surrounding heights on both sides of the river, angling for salmon, and riding the countryside, the Homes especially in their element, and collecting cattle and sheep from a wide swathe of Northumbrian territory. Watch was kept, of course, for any enemy arrival to assist Wark's people, but none appeared, presumably most of the local lords and squires, with their men, being down in the south, facing France.

It was to be hoped that Mary Tudor and Cardinal Pole got the message. Marie hoped also that Argyll and Huntly and the other great magnates recognised that the queen mother could act without their assistance or indeed approval.

She was, in fact, seeking to build up an alternative power group in the realm to counter the strength of these great nobles. Her aim was to create a national army. Not since the days of the Bruce had there been anything such in the land, all military action being dependent on the armed levies of the lords. France had such. Why not Scotland? It would cost money, of course, much money, to pay for a sufficiently large number of men always ready to carry out the royal commands. That meant taxation, which would require parliament's authority. But Dean Sinclair and his Archbishop Beaton of Glasgow declared that the Church would be prepared to back this need, with its great wealth, as a stabilising force in the nation, however strange it might seem for the clerics to be subsidising great numbers of armed men. But it would help to keep the proud lords in order and prevent them from dominating the scene. Marie was much gratified.

So, after Wark, she called a parliament. From the throne she herself proposed the formation of a national army, despite the sour looks of the Chancellor Huntly and other lords, but with the united support of the churchmen, both Catholic and Protestant, and the representatives of the cities and royal burghs, and of most of the shires commissioners, which guaranteed a majority vote, however odd it might seem for a woman to be advocating this new conception of a standing military establishment, aided and abetted by the divines. Many questions were asked, to be sure, as to what the army's men would do when there was no call for action. To which the reply was that it would be divided up throughout the realm, under commanders responsible to parliament to keep good order, especially along the Highland Line and in the Borders, and the Galloway and Solway areas. Also to aid city provosts and townsmen in maintaining order and putting down crime, robbery and violence.

That was a most notable, indeed momentous parliament, defining and proclaiming the rule of central authority, and greatly limiting the power of the nobility. Marie was fortunate in having the strong support of the man whom she had appointed Secretary of State, one Maitland of Lethington, a shrewd and far-sighted administrator. Also of Sir William Kirkcaldy of Grange, a noted soldier who had served in the wars of the Continent, famed for his tactical skills and bravery.

It had been a long time since parliament had accepted and agreed to a major increase in taxation, necessary to pay for all this, largely by augmented import and export duties, which did not hit the nobles, and which the commoners saw as eventually aiding their interests.

David Lindsay composed a ballad-play to celebrate it all, however scurrilous some of its asides. He called it *Ane Satyre of the Thrie Estaites*. The divines, whom he so scornfully castigated in these verses, demanded that the pages should be publicly burned; but Marie ensured that this was not done.

As it happened, soon after the parliament another was called for, this because King Henry of France, presumably because a sickness had suddenly struck him, sought that the proposed marriage of his son and heir, the Dauphin Francis, and Mary, young Queen of Scots, should be implemented forthwith. Mary was now in her sixteenth year, Francis eighteen months younger. But sufficiently old for a royal marriage.

Marie sent commissioners over to France to confirm the

arrangements, and ensure that Scotland's position was secure in this union of the crowns – for of course Francis would become King-Consort of Scotland and in due course King of France, Mary two queens. Archbishop Beaton, Bishop Reid of Orkney and the Earls of Cassillis and Rothes, with the Lords Fleming and Seton, were allotted this mission, David Lindsay going with them as Marie's personal representative.

They were suitably well received at the French court, where they found Queen Catherine de Medici all but ruling the land in the name of her sick husband, and persecuting direly the Calvinist reformers, a strong and dominant woman. The terms of the marriage settlement were agreed, with a dowry of four hundred thousand crowns provided for the bride.

The marriage was celebrated at the Cathedral of Notre-Dame in Paris by Cardinal Bourbon, the Guise brothers, including their own cardinal, more or less marginalised by the royal Bourbon family and Queen Catherine. There were murmurings at the French court, despite the seeming splendour and excellence of the occasion. Marie, learning of it, made plans for the fuller nuptials to be suitably celebrated at St Andrews, her brothers invited to attend.

But the flourish of the French occasion was abruptly overwhelmed by catastrophe. The Scots representatives had got only as far as Dieppe on their way home when first Bishop Reid of Orkney was seized by a choking ailment, and died. And two days later, on their ship, the Earl of Rothes was similarly stricken, and perished. Cassillis was then struck down likewise, and followed by the Lord Fleming. Some of their retinue also perished. Archbishop Beaton, Lord Seton and others survived, including David Lindsay. This dire and dumbfounding disaster could have been caused by some contamination of the food they had consumed; but there were whispers that it was poison, arranged by the Guise brothers in retaliation for their partial eclipse by Queen Catherine's Bourbons and her ambitions towards Scotland, a warning.

Marie was appalled when Lindsay told her of it all. She could not believe that her brothers were capable of it, and thought that Catherine de Medici was the more likely culprit if indeed it was poison. But to what advantage? These envoys had agreed to her son becoming King-Consort of Scotland; and one day he would be King of France also, and the two realms, so long in alliance, would be reigned over by husband and wife. What had she, Catherine, to gain by the deaths of these ambassadors?

Whatever the cause, with the nation mourning these so remarkable deaths, another death caused a different kind of apprehension in Scotland only shortly thereafter. Queen Mary Tudor passed away suddenly, in only her forty-third year; this meant the accession to the English throne of her half-sister, Elizabeth, and great upheavals, not only in England. For while Mary had been a fervid Catholic, her sister was as pronounced a Protestant. The two factions in Scotland were very aware of possible repercussions, Marie likewise.

However, Elizabeth Tudor sought to prevent outright religious warfare in her nation by skillfully retaining on her Privy Council no fewer than thirteen prominent Catholics, including Heath, the Archbishop of York, Paulett, Marquis of Winchester, with Clinton, the Lord Admiral. But she dismissed Cardinal Pole. She appointed seven others, strong Protestants, with William Cecil as Secretary of State, and Walsingham and Sackville to high office.

Scotland watched and waited. Was Protestant Elizabeth

to prove as much of a menace as had been Catholic Mary? Her prudent first appointments to power were reassuring however. She was popular with her common folk, as Mary had not been, which was probably a good sign.

Then there developed a new crisis, and this caused by Marie's own brothers. The Guises, by a military coup, seized Calais, the nearest French port to England and long held by the English. This aroused great anger in London and all but a declaration of war on France, even though Queen Catherine denied all responsibility. Elizabeth's ministers said that it must be retaken. Marie did not bless her brothers. She feared that an attack on Scotland might be mounted by way of retaliation, for Calais would not be easily retaken.

This made the creating of a national army the more urgent, and Marie set about its furtherance with vigour, appointing the justiciars of the various areas to recruit volunteers – all to be paid for by the churchmen, whatever the lords thought of it.

The response was good, many young men seeing joining as much to be preferred to ploughing and reaping and tending their fathers' flocks and herds. The Highlanders in especial flocked to the royal banner, and established their own infantry regiments, linked to the various clans and their allies. The Borderers also found it suitable actually to be paid for being in arms, and produced much cavalry. Unexpectedly good was the reaction from the cities and large towns, with soldiering appealing much more than toiling in markets and mills, carpentry and carpet-making. Marie had to approach the senior clergy for more moneys. Another parliament praised the initiative, although there was silence from the lords' benches. The assembly also agreed, by a fair majority, that the Dauphin of France, now wed to their queen, should be given the title of King of Scotland but *not* King of Scots, a nice distinction. The Great Seal of the Kingdom would have to be redesigned. A hopeful gesture was to be made by sending congratulations to the new Queen Elizabeth on her assumption of the throne as Protestant monarch, Marie in favour of this. She was becoming expert in balancing her religious convictions, or at least their rapport.

IO

Marie had long ached to go to France to see her daughter. And not only Mary, for her son Francis, Duke of Longueville, was all but a stranger to her now, he in his twenty-second year, married, and with his own little son. She felt guilty of neglecting him all the long interval, but amid her manifold responsibilities it could not have been avoided. Being regent for Mary in Scotland much restricted her opportunities for pursuing her interests elsewhere, especially with a religious reformation going on. And her Guise brothers were not the least of her problems. Now, after retaking Calais from the English, they were making the claim that their niece, Mary, Queen of Scots, should also be Queen of England, as well as being wed to the future King of France; for they held that Elizabeth Tudor was illegitimate, one of the late Henry's innumerable bastards, whereas *their* Mary, his sister's granddaughter, lawfully born, was the true heir to his throne. They had even devised a banner for her, incorporating the arms of Scotland, France and England.

In all this, as in so much else, Elizabeth acted with caution, heeding the good advice of William Cecil. To avoid possible war with France, which might have suited not a few of her lords, she went so far as to add her name to the Treaty of Cateau-Cambrésis, which ended the struggle between France and Spain, this as guarantor. And she sent the Bishop of Ely and the Lord William Howard to assure Marie of her desire for a lasting peace and co-operation with Scotland. Marie was only too glad to agree, and despatched Secretary Maitland and David Lindsay south to confirm it all. She ordered the fortress erected by D'Oysel at Eyemouth, threatening Berwick, be destroyed, as a gesture. And instructed that Admiral Wood's ships should stop attacking English privateers, this unless they actually caught these assailing Scots vessels.

All this peace promotion was not aided by John Knox who, after a spell in Geneva with the reforming Calvin, returned to Scotland even more fiery than ever, stirring up anti-Catholic enmity, which Marie was seeking to play down. He aroused the Edinburgh mob to hurl down the statue of St Giles, which stood beside the High Kirk of that name, and had it cast into the Nor' Loch which lay at the northern foot of the castle-rock. Not content with this, he had it dragged out again and smashed to pieces, in the name of reform, even though it was, as it were, the capital city's patron saint. Marie saw this as dangerous and likely to increase bitterness, even actual warfare between Holy Church and the Protestants. She had another statue of Giles created, and carried down the High Street and Canongate from the castle to Holyrood in a great procession of more moderate divines and canons and priests, she accompanying it with her royal guards and waving to the populace as indication of unity in the worship of Almighty God, hoping that it might keep the citizens from fighting each other as pro- and anti-Knox. Not a few of her advisers urged her to have this troublesome man arrested and imprisoned, some strong Catholics even advocating that he be burned at the stake for heresy; but she would have none of that. Was their Creator not the God of love, however aggressive was Master Knox? Her duty and mission was to maintain peace in her daughter's realm, despite such firebrands.

She was, none the less, determined to see her daughter – and if possible her son. She seized the chance when Knox made another visit to Calvin. She ordered the Lords of the Articles to act in her name and maintain peace, for hopefully no more than a couple of weeks, and had one of Wood's ships sail her to Dieppe, taking David Lindsay with her.

In Paris, it was sheer delight to see Mary at long last after so lengthy a parting. She was now no mere girl but a young woman and a beauteous one, of lively personality, sparkling of eye, comely of figure and vivaciously attractive. Beside her, the Dauphin Francis, poor man, made but a dull, all but feeble figure, dominated by his masterful mother, Queen Catherine de Medici, as indeed was her husband, Henry the Second. Catherine was a strange woman, not good-looking but with an aura of power and authority, daughter of the Florentine Prince Lorenzo. Marie got the impression that she did not greatly love her daughter-in-law, possibly jealous of her beauty and appeal to men.

Henry, however, made much of Marie's arrival, despite her Guise blood, which the royal house distrusted as overpowerful. He seemed eager to show how much he approved of his son's wife, whatever the attitude of his queen. He organised banquets, pageantry, sporting events, and on the fourth day a great tournament, to which he summoned most of the leading knights and paladins of the land, with Mary to act the queen of the occasion and present the prizes, this flourish also to celebrate the announcement of his two daughters' betrothals to King Philip of Spain and to Emmanuel, Duke of Savoy. Sir David

Lindsay was scheduled to compete with Count Louis of Mayenne.

Alas, it was not to be, any of it, save for the very first contest. For this, to lead off, King Henry himself was pitted against the Captain of Queen Mary's Scots Guard, Sir Gabriel Montgomery, a brother of the third Lord Montgomery of Eglinton. And, at only the second tilt, the Scot's lance by mischance slid up over the king's helmet and under the visor, to enter his left eye and into the brain, to his death.

That needless to say, was the end of all celebrations, marital and otherwise. After the funeral at Notre-Dame, instead of nuptials and betrothals attended by the greatest ones of Europe, Marie bade farewell to her daughter, so suddenly and tragically become Queen-Consort of France, however much under the direction of her mother-in-law Catherine.

A new era had begun, and for more than France.

Marie's return to Scotland was to find the land ringing with comment, wonder and shock over the latest pronouncement from Master John Knox. He had produced a pamphlet entitled *The First Blast of the Trumpet against the Monstrous Regiment of Women*, in which he declared that females were created by God to be subservient to men, and should never be elevated to the rule and governance of nations, it being males who were made in the image of God the Creator.

This diatribe and challenge represented all but high treason against the young queen and her regent mother – and also, to be sure, Queen Elizabeth of England, fellow Protestant as she might be; and for that matter Catherine de Medici who was now ruling France. Whatever else he

80

might be, Knox was scarcely tactful and concerned with his own wellbeing. In the outcry against this denunciation, its author fled to a land where no female held sway, to the Swiss republics of Zurich and Geneva which had successfully escaped from the sway of the Emperor. Here Heinrich Bullinger now held undisputed power, and Knox could feel secure to issue further controversial pronouncements.

Marie was thankfully quit of him meantime, but recognised that he would be back.

A more immediate problem was her daughter's position. The new young King Francis was scarcely able to compete with his formidable mother, so that Mary found herself queen only in name. But she was a spirited young woman, and prevailed upon him to issue a resounding statement, without consultation with Catherine, this making all Scots and French nationals co-citizens of both countries, a most notable and unprecedented situation, which had far-reaching effects in more than mere relations; for it meant that all trade between the two realms could be carried out without import and export duties, harbour-dues were not required for their ships, and any attack by English privateers was an act of war against both; also nationals of both could join merchants' and workers' guilds and associations in either land. The Auld Alliance had never been so strong and complete. Marie rejoiced, having suggested it to her daughter. The commercial and other benefits applied equally to Protestant and Catholic, so it had a unifying effect in both kingdoms.

In the circumstances Catherine de Medici could not complain, however wary she was about Mary's influence on her son.

Marie received a letter from her daughter announcing that while out hunting she had been knocked off her horse by an overhanging tree branch, but was not grievously hurt. She also mentioned that her mother-in-law, Queen Catherine, sat at her side on all occasions – this indicating that the Medici was reluctant to relinquish power to the new young queen. Marie did not like the sound of that.

She was having increasing problems nearer at hand. Seeking to steer a moderate course between the Protestant and Catholic factions, she was greatly upset by a mob of the citizens of Perth sacking the monasteries of the Black and Grey Friars and the Carthusian Priory, or Charterhouse, and stealing all that they could lay their hands on, leaving only the blackened walls standing, this after Knox who had returned to Scotland, had preached one of his inflammatory sermons in the St John's Kirk there – although even he condemned this spoliation as shameful. Marie felt that something had to be done to curb this sort of behaviour, and emphasise the rule of law in the land. She summoned Arran, now styling himself Duke of Chatelherault, with Atholl and Argyll; and together with D'Oysel, the French commander, led all personally for Perth.

However, on the way, they learned that a group of nobles and lairds calling themselves the Lords of the Congregation were preparing to prevent the regent from entering the town; and when word was brought that these had been joined by the Cunninghame Earl of Glencairn with twelve hundred horse and thirteen hundred foot, discretion was indicated. She sent Argyll and her own stepson, the Lord James Stewart, a bastard of her husband, who as Prior of St Andrews, although no cleric, had gone to France and had been present at the marriage of Mary and the Dauphin. Now he was back in Scotland.

Terms were come to with Glencairn and the Lords of the

Congregation, and it was agreed that their forces should be dispersed, for her part Marie accepting that no French garrison, under D'Oysel, should hold Perth. A parliament must be held to try to resolve difficulties.

That assembly, held in Edinburgh Castle, was a noisy and unruly one, Huntly, the Chancellor still, left in no doubt that the majority present were of the reformed persuasion. Marie, from the throne, sought to aid him in keeping order of a sort, but not to let her own religious preferences become over-evident. The clerics present were all of the old faith, of course, as were many of the nobles; but the representatives of the cities, shires and royal burghs tended to be in the other camp. And the Lords of the Congregation made their presence felt in no uncertain fashion. Marie judged that voting would be apt to be almost equal on most issues – which was a recipe for unhelpful results and compromises. Knox, among the spectators in the minstrels' gallery, although he had no authorised part to play in the proceedings, was probably the most vocal man there, however much Huntly sought to silence him, even threatening to have him ejected from the building.

Even the non-religious business was most evidently affected by partisan adherence, and gaining a fair decision on matters secular was difficult, however inoffensive to either side. Marie more than once had to rise from her chair and stand, as indication that she would leave the hall, and so end the session, unless order was restored.

Much of the debate, if that it could be called, was concerned with the royal situation. Mary was now Queen of France as well as Queen of Scots, and this brought the position of her husband into question. King-Consort of Scotland he might be, but definitely not King of Scots. The ancient matrilineal succession theme of Albannach times was brought forth, and the danger of Scotland degenerating into a mere appendage of France emphasised. The Auld Alliance must not be allowed to become more than that; and with the regent French, the queen half French and her husband King of France, there was that danger.

And there were Elizabeth Tudor's situation and attitudes to be considered. In the event of Mary dying without a child to heir her Scots throne, Elizabeth might well claim it. Was there in fact a legitimate closer claimant, other than the feeble Chatelherault? At all costs, that must be nullified. An English queen on Scotland's throne! Knox's *Monstrous Regiment of Women* was cited. And there were these whispers that young King Francis of France was incapable of fathering a child. It was accepted that Chatelherault, not present as usual, was not to be considered; but that one of the late monarch's bastards might have to be accepted, however illegitimate – preferably the Lord James Stewart, who was the son of Flaming Janet Kennedy, daughter of Cassillis, he who had married the heiress of the elderly and failing Earl of Mar and would gain that title in due course. He might be the best nominee for the crown. It was all a most delicate and awkward situation, not least for Marie sitting there on the throne.

In the end, the main issues were left for the Lords of the Articles to consider, and recommend decisions for a further parliament, with Queen Mary's own views to be discovered, this being left to her royal mother to ascertain. She was young and spirited, and who knew that might be her future destination and destiny?

So another visit to France for the regent appeared to be indicated.

Delay there had to be, however. The Catholic–Protestant animosity grew ever more violent, and Marie's efforts to steer a moderate course involved her in almost daily concern.

Moreover, her own health was suffering, whether from stress, infection or merely the years taking their toll. A swelling of the ankles was the first sign of trouble, and when she consulted a physician, he said that it could be dropsy. She sought to ignore this, for weeks; but when she began to have spells of breathlessness, and this was attributed to dropsy also, she recognised that she would have to take it seriously. She was not going to let it interfere with her duties as regent if she could help it; but she would have to limit her journeyings around the country, her hunting and hawking and other outdoor activities in some degree. Her daughter needed her greatly, Scotland needed her, and the religious situation needed her, she judged. This was no time to become any sort of invalid.

She well recognised that the reformers and the vehement supporters of Holy Church must not be allowed to tear the realm apart. The Lords of the Congregation were becoming ever more vociferous, and one, Erskine of Dun, beginning to outdo even John Knox, not in sermonising and maledictions but in urging his fellow lairds and nobles to take violent action. The last parliament had degenerated into all but chaotic confrontation, and another might well do likewise. Marie decided to call a different sort of convention that March of 1559, this at Edinburgh, a great meeting of the clergy, *only* the clergy, but those of all shades and aspects of worship, from bishops and abbots to parish priests and reformed divines. She herself would preside, and seek to maintain a balance and attain some sort of agreement.

She held it, not at Holyrood, which might seem to favour the prelates, but at the High Kirk of St Giles in the High Street, the largest in the city, this necessary to seat all the many attending. Knox and Erskine of Dun were present, of course, and glaring at Archbishop Beaton and other senior clerics. But Marie, in her opening speech, declared that they were all there as seeking to enhance the many aspects of the worship of the God of love, and that while discussion and debate were called for, polemics and diatribes were not. They were there to reach agreement that preferred forms of worship should be open to all law-abiding subjects of the crown, and no forms and services imposed on unwilling churchgoers. Mutual understanding and forbearance were what was called for. She would dismiss the convention if this was not adhered to, and the attenders, who had come from far and wide, would find their presence fruitless. They were there to further the better worship of God the Father, God the Son and God the Holy Spirit, in the differing ways that people would wish.

She was heard in careful silence.

Marie went on. "Since reform in Holy Church has been felt by many to be necessary, and this has led to the present clash and disharmony, I will call upon the protesters and seekers of change to make known *their* proposals and requirements first. Who so speaks?"

Knox was rising when Erskine, at his side, laid a hand on his arm, restraining him.

"*I* seek to do so, in the name of all who would see betterment carried out in the Church," he said. "There must be an end to abuses, the appointment of ignorant men to high office, the amassing of wealth and lands by prelates, the parishes being neglected and many kirks in ruins while palaces flourish. Reforming priests and divines must be permitted to pray and baptise in the tongue of the people, not only in the Latin. And such improvers to be able to hold their own convocations or assemblies. That, and have like-minded ministers to teach and lecture in the universities. Much else – but these are the prime concerns of those who advocate reform." He sat.

At his side Knox jumped up, not to be silenced. "I demand, in the name of the Almighty, that all acts of parliament in which clerics were given permission to proceed against so-called heretics should be abolished. And any accusations against reformers, which are contested in law, should be brought before fair temporal judges and not in the shameful and diabolical prelatical courts!" He raised a fisted hand. "And God's curse on all who would stand in the way of this cleansing of rogues!" That was a shout.

Marie stood, and pointed at him authoritatively. "Enough, sir! Watch your words!" She turned, and gestured towards the senior clerics. "My lord Archbishop?" she invited.

Beaton of Glasgow rose. The other archbishopric, of St Andrews, was at this time vacant, although the Lord James Stewart, Marie's stepson, called himself prior thereof, despite being no cleric.

"Holy Church in this land, in Christ's name and in all

loyalty to His Holiness the Pope, requires certain ordinances," he said. "One, that no opposition to the Mass being conducted in parish churches be permitted. Two, that prayers for the saints' intervention be not banned. Three, that . . ." He got no further, uproar from the Protestant divines, led by Knox, drowning his voice.

"I also say that prayers for the dead should be said. Moreover, that any lords and lairds of the so-called Protestant persuasion be prohibited by law from ejecting ministers from parishes because of their adherence to Catholic services and ordinances," he went on.

That was as far as he got. Erskine interrupted. "In the name of the people of this land, I declare to this prelate, and all others, that bishops should be elected, with the consent of the gentry of the diocese; and the parish priests by the votes of the parishioners."

That produced scorn, even laughter from the Catholics. Marie saw that no advantage was to be gained by further talk and assertions this day by these antagonists; it could not be called debate. Yet they represented the strongly held views of a great many in the nation. What was she to do? They must somehow agree to co-exist in as near acceptance of each other as was possible. The authority of parliament alone could demand and enforce this. She there and then ended the meeting by announcing that she would call one, and gave the necessary forty days' notice. That said, she dismissed the convention with the word that she would call the parliament at Stirling, as central and allowing the best attendance from the Highlands, which were largely of the Catholic persuasion.

Forty days. Much would happen in forty days, and did. The Lords of the Congregation urged the Protestant faction to rise in fullest strength and demonstrate the will of the people, themselves leading, so that the summoned parliament would have no doubts as to it. Throughout the Lowlands turmoil resulted, in the cities and towns especially, where the reformers were strongest. Dundee excelled itself, bands of its citizens marching up Tay the dozen miles to Scone to attack the abbey there, crowning-place of the Scots monarchy as it was, casting down what they called idolatrous monuments. Edinburgh declared itself in favour of the Congregation, the folk surging down to occupy Holyrood, only the impregnable citadel remaining unassailed. In Perth the monasteries of the Grey and Black Friars and even the Carthusian shrine which held the ashes of James the First were sacked. Marie's palace of Linlithgow was threatened by a mob, and she retired to the strong castle of Dunbar, on the east coast, to await the hoped-for arrival of a French fleet which D'Oysel had called for, this to threaten England – for there was no question but that the militant Protestants were being encouraged by Elizabeth Tudor, or at least her advisers. In the circumstances, Marie's efforts at steering a moderate and neutral course in the religious controversy were difficult to maintain. She even began to wonder whether she might have to sail for France, unsuitable as this would be for her daughter's regent in Scotland.

However, that was not necessary. A group of earls, led by Argyll, Protestants as they were but largely with Highland connections, recognised that the Congregationalists were overdoing it with their rabble-rousing, and in fact hindering the reforming cause. They sent an envoy to Marie at Dunbar, assuring her of their loyalty to the crown and to the regency, and declaring that they would assemble their strength to counter the activities of the trouble-makers and ensure that when the parliament met it would not be under extreme Protestant threat, nor that of unruly citizen mobs. If the regent would return up Forth by ship to Stirling, they would be there to impose law and order on the land in her name.

Thankfully Marie accepted their offer of aid, and sailed for Stirling in a local vessel.

There she found Argyll, the Earl Marischal, Glencairn, Montrose and other powerful lords, with Erskine of Dun, to her surprise, they having gained the latter's agreement to try to control the more rampant Protestants, to the advantage of their own cause. She agreed with them that she and they should go to St Andrews, the ecclesiastical capital of the realm, and there issue a joint statement.

This proved to be a satisfactory meeting, the various factions now very much aware of the dangers of war. So a declaration was made, Erskine of Dun and other prominent reformers signing it, together with the earls including Catholic Huntly and Menteath. Oddly, one of the uniting factors was the fear of French troops under D'Oysel, with the aid of their naval force, creating military domination in the name of young Queen Mary. Marie found herself promising that this must not happen, and thus acting as a bridge between the sides. Thus, in some measure, D'Oysel held the key to peace, a key which she, and only she could use to good effect.

Sadly Marie's health was deteriorating rapidly now, her dropsy grievously afflicting her and, however much she fought it, inevitably affecting her ability to act as she would.

Unfortunately John Knox saw the situation as demanding violent action. He had won over the citizens of Dundee. Now he went to Edinburgh, and by his fiery eloquence, warning of French armed domination under D'Oysel, succeeded in rousing the capital to armed rebellion, he threatening to go to Glasgow also and do the like.

Marie, sick as she was, decided that she must somehow negotiate a state of mutual acceptance between the two main sides before the Stirling parliament, however difficult Knox's behaviour made this. Too unwell to ride, and advised that it would be unsafe for her to enter Edinburgh itself, from Leith, in the circumstances, she had a vessel pick her up at Boroughstoneness, the port for Linlithgow, and carry her down Forth to Prestonpans, some ten miles east of the capital, there to meet representatives of the city, the Lords of the Congregation, and others – but not Knox himself who, when invited, refused as "supping with the Devil"!

Marie, at Prestonpans, declared that she would restrain D'Oysel from military action so long as the Congregationalists did not call on Elizabeth of England to send them aid. Free worship would be allowed to all, with no attempt to impose the Catholic faith on parish ministers; but the Mass must be freely administered where desired, and no ban put upon its celebration at her court, and no Protestant preacher, Knox or other, to hold forth in her presence.

She hoped that she would be sufficiently well to attend the parliament at Stirling, now soon to be held, which she ought to be able to reach by boat up Forth.

She did so, well realising that it would be the last parliament she would preside over. Thereafter her daughter would have to come herself, or else create another regent. Who? Chatelherault, always feeble, was getting feebler, although his son, now using the style of Earl of Arran, was ambitious. And the Lord James Stewart, illegitimate as he might be, was said to be talking of succeeding to the regency, even putting himself forward for the crown itself, as more suitable than having Mary of France as monarch of Scotland. Marie wondered and wondered. Would Mary choose to come back to Scotland? She was all but a Frenchwoman, but unhappy at being dominated by Catherine de Medici, and might elect so do to.

That parliament, inevitably, was again almost wholly concerned with the religious situation, and Marie found it all trying indeed. For too long she had been seeking to cope with this unsuitable, indeed shameful battle between the two forms of Christian worship, and to ensure if possible that the national will prevailed. Now, a sick woman, and weary of it all, she came to the conclusion that she would be better in that other realm beyond the grave, where she would not be a queen or regent or anything of a ruler of awkward folk but a humble worshipper, closer to Christ Himself, the loving lord of all. The sooner the better as far as she was concerned. But, for Scotland . . . ?

The parliament was all talk of improper ceremonies and idolatrous abuses, the clear majority being anti-Catholic, with frequent glares being directed at the throne.

So be it, she told herself. She had done what she could. Let others decide the future, preferably the loving Creator. She was thankful when she could rise and leave. Who would sit there, at the next parliament?

Marie de Guise died only a month later, in her forty-fifth year, a woman glad to go, her faith in the hereafter un- faltering, and assured of love triumphant.

POSTCRIPT

Marie de Guise died on the eleventh day of June 1560, but her funeral was postponed in extraordinary fashion. Six weeks after her passing, a service and oration was conducted for her at Notre-Dame, in Paris; but it was not until 9 October, after lying in state at Edinburgh Castle, that her body was brought to France, this on account of Knox and the other Protestant divines disapproving of the obsequies that would be observed there. The corpse was taken to Fécamp in Normandy in March 1561; and in July removed to Reims, where at last it was buried at the convent of St Pierre, where her sister was abbess, after an elaborate funeral service, Mary, Queen of Scots attending.

What Marie, looking down on it, thought of all this is best left to the imagination.

Part Two

12

Mary Stewart, Queen of Scots and, since the death of her father-in-law the year before, Queen of France also, was now aged eighteen years, and finding herself in a very strange, indeed dangerous position, on account of her powerful mother-in-law Catherine de Medici's resentment that this young woman should be Queen of France instead of herself. Catherine did not seek to hide this; and there were even rumours at court that she might have Mary poisoned, or alternatively her own young son Francis, whom she despised as a weakling, this to remove any threat to her own power. Moreover, Catherine was far from beautiful, whereas Mary was, a matter of concern where women were at odds.

The queen-dowager was however spared having to get rid of her sickly and strangely wizened son, for Francis, after periods of inability to speak, died of natural causes in December 1560, leaving Mary a widow. Their marriage had never been fully consummated.

Mary's Guise uncles were not backward in seeking to arrange her remarriage, it even being suggested that she might be wed to one of *them*, the Grand Prior Francis of Guise, although papal dispensation would have to be gained for this. Mary herself was much against it, revealing herself to be as determined a young woman as she was attractive. There was also talk of her being betrothed to Don Carlos of Spain, heir to the great Spanish empire; but accounts of this sixteen-year-old's state of person and character were scarcely encouraging. He was as feeble a possible husband as had been the late Francis, tiny of body, allegedly weighing only just over five stones, not exactly a cripple but twisted of build, and suffering from epilepsy. Mary was not going to be tied to any such unfortunate. She determined that, since she was Queen of Scots, she should go back to the land of her birth, and seek to end all such dynastic machinations. In that remote-seeming realm, as monarch, she ought to be free to make her own choices and get away from the sway of Catherine de Medici.

This decision was furthered by the arrival in France of two Scots envoys from opposing camps, John Leslie, Bishop of Ross, representing the Catholic faction, and the Lord James Stewart, Mary's illegitimate half-brother, a strong Protestant. These two, although for very different reasons, urged Mary's prompt return to Scotland. The bishop assured her that at Aberdeen she would find twenty thousand armed men, assembled by the Catholic Highland lords and chiefs, to ensure her security on the Scots throne; while the Lord James declared that on his way to France he had called upon Queen Elizabeth Tudor at London, and gained her acceptance that there should be a renewal of the Treaty of Edinburgh affirming perpetual peace between England, Scotland and France.

She declared that she was ready to go, and was told that James Hepburn, Earl of Bothwell, who had assumed the new style of Lord High Admiral of Scotland in succession to Sir Andrew Wood, would come to Calais to fetch her.

So, on the twelfth day of August 1561 Mary embarked on Bothwell's great galleon, with her courtiers, including four Guise uncles, and the four Marys who had come with her to France all those years ago, Seton, Beaton, Fleming and Livingstone, escorted by three other vessels. It made an emotional departure, Mary in tears repeating, "Adieu, France! Adieu, France!" and hoping that the foggy conditions did not presage any doubtful future.

Mary had, as a courtesy, applied to Queen Elizabeth for the usual safe-conduct, but this request had been ignored. Nevertheless, all the six hundred miles northwards to Scotland, English vessels hovered around the Scots ships, the notorious privateers which made the Norse Sea such a menace to merchant shipping. However, none sought to attack, no doubt warned not to by London. The voyage, although slow because of the lack of wind and the mists, was completed in five days and nights. Mary was glad of her four namesakes always close to her, because of the attentions of the handsome and romantically minded Bothwell with whom they had to be cooped up. He had brought a group of musicians with him to liven the occasion.

In due course they entered the Firth of Forth, and all exclaimed at the spectacular flourish of the bird-haunted cliffs of the Isle of May, the sheer soaring heights of the Craig of Bass, the isolated conical peak of North Berwick Law, and ahead of them the lion-like profile of Edinburgh's Arthur's Seat, all a dramatic introduction to Scotland famed for its eye-catching scenery.

At Leith, the port for the capital, they were welcomed by a great and distinguished company, while Edinburgh Castle, two miles distant, thundered out a continuous cannonade, re-echoed from the surrounding hills. Mary had not forgotten how hilly Scotland was, although when she had left, those long years ago, it had been beneath higher heights than these, the mountains of Arran and Kintyre and the Clyde estuary, from Dumbarton.

The Leith harbour-master was rowed out in his barge to lead in the queen's ship, with him the Secretary of State Maitland.

Bothwell's vessel was guided in, to moor at the quayside under the towering tenements and lower warehouses of the port, where Argyll, Huntly, the High Constable, the Earl Marischal and Lord James Stewart waited to welcome the monarch. Gangways were lowered for the passengers to land.

Mary was the first to descend. She paused, halfway down, to the cheers of the waiting throng and crowds of the common folk massed behind. She was dressed all in black, with white silken scarf and cuffs, unlike the rest of the company, since she was still in mourning for her late husband Francis. She smiled and waved to all, however, lovely, radiant. Then she lifted her skirts to negotiate the cross-bars of the planking, revealing shapely legs and ankles, she not unaware of her femininity.

The cheering continued, even the cannonade not drowning it.

At the foot of the gangway her half-brother, the Lord James, came forward, the first to greet her as she stepped on to Scottish ground. Never before had a queen-regnant done so, save for the Maid of Norway reaching only Orkney. She embraced and kissed him. Behind her came Bothwell and the Guise uncles, with the four Marys.

James Stewart presented the other welcoming notables, commencing with Argyll and his fellow earls, the bishops, lords, Wardens of the Marches, and the provost of Edinburgh, Mary gracious, obviously happy to be thus received in her native land.

They all moved to the tall gabled house of Andrew Lamb, a prosperous Leith merchant, where refreshments were laid on for all, before the ride up to the city, horses provided.

How many years since she had been here? Thirteen? She did not remember Holyrood Abbey and its palace wing, but Arthur's Seat, towering high above it, was etched in her mind. Edinburgh's castle-fortress on its rock was the royal seat, but the abbey was much more comfortable and convenient, and the monks ever hospitable. Bonfires of welcome blazed, and the common folk thronged the streets, waving and cheering.

That evening, clad magnificently in crimson and gold silk, Mary demonstrated her joy at being back in her northern kingdom, after feasting, by dancing and singing, for she had a fine, tuneful voice. Also she announced that she was celebrating her return to Scotland by creating her good brother, the Lord James, Earl of Moray. And she spoke of her gratitude and love for her late mother, the Queen Marie de Guise, who had for so long ruled this land effectively and at a difficult period of religious controversies. She was also glad to introduce her uncles, the Guise dukes, to them all.

She asked about Master John Knox, of whom she had heard much – she did not declare the execration of his name in France, where his fulminations against the Catholic faith were notorious – and was told that he was now minister of the High Kirk of St Giles here, which Mary had always heard of as a cathedral, but not now apparently. Argyll, although a Protestant himself, revealed that Knox, as chief divine of the capital, had been invited to attend the welcoming company at Leith, but had declared that he had no time to indulge in such frivolities. Mary was warned. Bothwell also told her that she would have to curb the activities of the Lords of the Congregation, who had been such a plague to her mother. Although these higher-born ones looked down on Knox as an up-jumped farmer's son, they were themselves almost equally hostile to what they called the popish oligarchy, and were bound to make trouble for the new royal regime.

Mary decided that she must seek to form some sort of link to bridge the gap between herself, with the Catholic community, and these diehard Protestants for the sake of the realm's weal. She would start with Knox himself. She requested, not ordered, him to come to see her at Holyrood.

The new Earl of Moray, the Lord James Stewart, was the only witness of this momentous occasion. Mary greeted the divine, a stern-faced man in his late forties, with a long flowing beard and burning eyes, as amiably as she was able, but did not fail to remind him of his blast against the Monstrous Regiment of Women.

"Sir," she said, smiling. "As one of the weak, frail and foolish creatures you declare to be unsuitable to conduct any sort of rule in a land, I greet you. It seems that our loving God has decreed that I should serve as sovereign of this realm, female as I am, or He would have made my royal father produce a son instead of myself, no? Or would you prefer that my good-brother here, the Lord James, should occupy the throne?"

Knox, unable to condone illegitimacy, inclined his hairy head. "What I would prefer is of no moment," he declared. "God's will be done. But so long as Your Grace behaves with due regard to the Almighty's ordinances, I must be content to live under you as Paul was to live under Nero!"

"Nero! That is scarcely a suitable image for a Christian queen, I think? But I rejoice that you, and your like, accept my rule—"

"So long as you are guided by *men* of sufficient worth in the sight of God!" he interrupted her. He distinctly emphasised that word "men".

"Would you, sir, have subjects defy and rise against their lawful monarch because she is a woman? Should my people obey others who would act contrary to myself because I am a female?"

"If so they judge God's will. As represented by Holy Kirk."

"Holy Kirk? What if we see Holy Kirk differently? *I* see it as based on Rome, you as certainly not. Whose conscience should prevail? The born monarch's, or yours, Master Knox?"

"Conscience requires knowledge," he asserted. "And, I fear, of right knowledge you have none!"

They gazed at each other, Mary's bosom heaving with indignation and frustration, Knox stroking his lengthy beard, assured in his divine authority.

The Lord James saw fit to intervene, this confrontation unprofitable as it was unsuitable, impasse reached. He spoke up.

"Master Knox, Her Grace is to make a royal progress through the city in but an hour's time. Much ceremonial is planned . . ."

"So long as it is not popish diablerie!" Knox declared. And with a curt nod, no bow, he took his departure.

"Do not judge all reformers by his like," Moray advised. "Master Knox is a law unto himself."

"He sees himself as the voice of the Almighty, I judge!"

"As does His Holiness of Rome, no?"

They left it at that.

Shortly thereafter Mary set out on her especial celebratory procession through the city, conducted by the provost and magistrates, Secretary Maitland and the Abbot of Holyrood. Up the Canongate they walked, to its Tolbooth, where fifty citizens awaited them, dressed as Moors, with blackened faces, legs and arms, in yellow taffeta costumes, these to dance on a stage to rhythmic chanting. A little further up, four fair virgins represented the four natural virtues, prudence, temperance, fortitude and justice. And still further, at the Butter Tron, a child descended from a sailcloth shroud painted to resemble a cloud, to present to the queen a Bible and psalter, this in the Scots tongue, not in Latin. At the Mercat Cross, four more virgins cupped out wine from barrels to offer to the queen and all others, this inevitably producing something of a scramble and much noise. On up the Lawnmarket, with cheering crowds all the way, they came to the tourney-ground at the approach to the castle, where were waiting jousters, wrestlers, jugglers and archers to display their skills, this amid the deafening bombilation of cannon-fire. The constable of the citadel presented the keys thereof at the gatehouse, and Mary, touching them, returned them to him, her acknowledgement lost in the din, all indeed coughing because of the smoke billowing down in the wind.

Within the fortress, Mary was taken up to a high point of the rock to visit the chapel of Saint Margaret, queen to Malcolm Canmore, she who had all but single-handed converted the ancient Columban monastic Church to the Roman Catholic one; and mother of King David, who had built all the abbeys out of the English gold gained by marrying the greatest heiress of that realm. Some of these fanes were now in part ruin, thanks to the hammers of the reformers, to Mary's distress. But this little chapel, secure within the fortress, was untouched; and Mary duly knelt before the altar to pay her respects and devotions, watched by her Protestant companions, features carefully controlled.

Mary wondered how her mother had for so long ruled successfully over a kingdom riven thus by religious strife.

All this was just the beginning of it. For three weeks she remained at Holyrood, visiting all parts of the capital and its surroundings, hawking around Arthur's Seat and Duddingston Loch, riding to explore the Braid, Blackford and Pentland Hills, and down into the Borderland, being entertained by the lords and lairds and abbots, loving the land if not necessarily all its owners, and rejoicing that she should be queen thereof, determined to seek to heal the controversies that were tearing her kingdom apart.

Then with James and Maitland she embarked on a wider tour of inspection, and to show herself to her subjects and her caring for them. She went to Linlithgow, where she had been born in her mother's dower-house by its loch; then on to Stirling, its castle the ancient seat of her forebears, worshipping at the abbey of Cambuskenneth, this where Bruce had received the surrender of the English lords after their defeat at Bannockburn. Then to Perth where, despite anti-Catholic pageantry, she was presented with a golden heart-shaped casket filled with gold pieces. At Dundee she was accorded a warm reception whatever its very Protestant reputation; and from there across the Tay to St Andrews, where James was still nominal prior, he having at one time proposed to take up a clerical career before the reform fever struck him.

She had another destination now, also in Fife. Falkland Palace had long been the royal hunting-seat, set below the twin peaks of the Lomond Hills, and she had never been there. She was especially eager to see the place, for it had a notable connection with her father. As a youth, he had escaped from the clutches of the Earl of Angus, his step-father, at Stirling, disguised as a stable-boy and found his way to Falkland, where he hid for weeks, this in 1528. It became thereafter his favourite residence; and here, after the rout of Solway Moss and the death of his favourite, Oliver Sinclair, he retired, turned his face to the wall, and died. And, long before that, in 1402, Robert the Third's son and heir was imprisoned by his uncle, the Duke of Albany, ambitious for the throne, and would have starved to death had not a kindhearted woman, employed as a wet-nurse in the township, fed him through the opening of a shot-hole in the walling with fragments of oatcake and with milk from her breasts squirted down a length of reed. All this appealed to Mary's romantic mind, and she must see the place.

With James and Maitland she rode westwards, the higher twin peaks of the Lomonds beckoned them on, known as the Paps of Fife, prominent indeed. At the northern foot of the eastern hill nestled the little burgh of Falkland, with its palace nearby, no large establishment – indeed apt to be insufficiently roomy to house the royal court and guests, so that the less important ones had to be sent to Cupar for lodging.

Mary was enchanted with Falkland and its surround-ings, much open woodland ideal for deer-hunting as well as being picturesque, and the heights above famed for the stalking of stags, this done afoot, as distinct from pursuing them on horseback; not that Mary had ever attempted anything such. James offered to teach her the skills of it, if so she felt inclined, despite the fact that it was not normally a sport for women, crawling about on their stomachs and less than convenient for their anatomy. Falkland, she decided, would be a favoured destination for her hereafter.

She got back to Edinburgh to find the English envoy, Sir Ralph Sadler, with a message from his Queen Elizabeth proposing a meeting of the two female monarchs, in the interests of lasting peace between the realms, and declaring that she would welcome Mary at her London court. This pleased Mary well enough, but not her advisers, who asserted that for her to go to London would seem as though she were the lesser in importance. Let any meeting be held halfway between the two capitals, perhaps at York, where the archepiscopal palace would make a suitable venue.

John Knox, however, inveighed against any such meeting wherever it was held, declaring the Tudor to be a she-devil, Protestant as she might claim to be. Indeed he preached to that effect from the pulpit of St Giles.

Whether Elizabeth heard of this last, or merely was offended at Mary's reluctance to attend her court, she indicated displeasure, and any meeting was put off meantime.

Mary was disappointed, an opportunity for accord lost; but took her councillors' advice against any appearance at London.

13

As well, perhaps, for whatever reason, that Mary did not go south the following autumn, for serious trouble broke out nearer home. The Gordon Earl of Huntly, the Chancellor, the leading Catholic noble, was the cause. His eldest son, the Lord Gordon, for some disagreement, attacked and seriously wounded the Lord Ogilvie in Edinburgh, and claiming lordly rights was brought before the sovereign, who warded him in Stirling Castle, or at least ordered him so to be. But on his way there, he escaped from his escort and fled to his father's northern territories; and gathering a thousand Gordon horsemen, defied the royal authority, Huntly supporting him.

This, against all the laws of the land, could not be overlooked; and the Lord James was given the task of bringing the Gordons to heel. It so happened that he and Huntly had a quarrel anyway, for now James was made Earl of Mar and Moray, and Huntly had possessed himself of certain of the Moray lands while that latter earldom was in abeyance and was refusing to give them up. James, of martial character, declared that he was going to retake them, by force of arms if necessary.

Mary, anxious to prevent what could well amount to civil war, decided to go north herself to seek to settle this dispute amicably. Huntly invited her to come to his palatial seat of Strathbogie; but she, perceiving this as restricting her from taking any necessary steps against *his* interests, elected to use the hitherto unvisited royal castle of Inverness.

However, when she arrived at the northern capital, it was to find its castle occupied by Huntly's men, and the gates shut against her, royal hold as it was. On being commanded to open, in the queen's name, the captain thereof declared that he took his orders from the Lord Gordon, Huntly's eldest son, and until he was so instructed, could not yield it, even to the monarch.

This amounted to no less than outright rebellion, even treason. James, there with his half-sister, asserted that he would raise the great manpower of Moray and Mar, both comparatively near at hand, to bring these Gordons to their senses. Mary was doubtful of the wisdom of this, since it would result almost inevitably in major battle. But Argyll and Maitland, with her, said that a demonstration of royal authority was much called for. She could not deny it, in the circumstances.

Faced with this situation, and not to seem to retire south in the face of such challenge, Mary agreed to a siege of Inverness Castle, declaring that she herself would direct it and adding that although she was no man to know what life was like to lie of a night in the field and wear jack and knapsack, she could act something of the soldier if necessary.

While James was raising the Moray men, and Argyll collecting clansmen from the nearby Highlands, Mary went to lodge in the Bishop of Moray's palace at Spynie, near Elgin. While there, word was brought to her by none other than Sir John Gordon, Huntly's second son, that his elder brother, the Lord Gordon, would yield up Inverness Castle on condition that he was not in any way punished, was allowed to go free and join his father at Strathbogie.

Mary found herself liking this young Sir John, a handsome and lively character who behaved towards her with marked gallantry. She told him that if his father would disband his forces and withdraw his demand for a Catholic uprising, she, a Catholic herself, would overlook his call to arms, and so peace would be restored in the north.

The situation appeared to be on the way to a satisfactory conclusion. However, Huntly made declaration that he would not disperse his host until the Lord James renounced his claims to much of the earldom of Moray which he, Huntly, looked upon as his own. James in no way would consider this; and Mary, having created him Earl of Moray and Mar, could scarcely command it. She had so to inform this Sir John Gordon, who was acting go-between, to that young man's grievous disappointment – for he was clearly much enjoying this relationship with the lovely queen, and was indeed becoming all but romantic about it.

Whatever his son's attitude to Mary might be, Huntly's was otherwise. He mustered more of his manpower from his wide domains, and fortified his castles of Auchindoun and Findlater, as well as Strathbogie. He began to march for Aberdeen in strength, presumably in the hope of seizing the queen herself, to which she had retired from Spynie.

James, Argyll, Atholl and Morton accepted the challenge, and however reluctant was Mary herself to see outright warfare develop, that began to seem inevitable.

They too marched to meet the Gordons, taking the queen with them.

Reports said that Huntly was approaching from Strathbogie, by Kennethmont, and had crossed the Don near Alford, this about thirty miles west of Aberdeen. With some two thousand men the royal force headed up Deeside, aiming to gain a position on the south bank of that river, which would be to the Gordons' disadvantage in having to cross it, against opposition, to reach them. Lord James, who had all but authoritatively taken command, sent a contingent under Atholl northwards, to present threat to Huntly's flank in the Skene and Dunecht area.

This strategy proved effective, in that Huntly divided his force, sending Lord Gordon to cope with it, and himself choosing to occupy the high ground of a long, isolated ridge just north of the Dee, in the Banchory vicinity, this named Corrichie.

James was certainly not going to attempt to climb that hill to challenge the enemy. Argyll and Atholl could assail it from more lofty ground to the east and behind. He would let Huntly do any attacking southwards. Admittedly then his charging cavalry could thunder down the steep slope upon them. But the ground was wet and boggy at the foot. He could use this. He arranged his men in a great semi-circle around this muddy area, and awaited events.

And events there were. Huntly, the Cock o' the North as he was styled, had the considerably larger force, having mustered his neighbouring allies, Leslies, Forbeses and Frasers; and although Mary's company included many great lords, the Earls of Argyll, Atholl, the Marischal, Morton, as well as James of Moray and Mar, these were far from their own grounds and had not much of their own strength with them, whereas the Gordon was based on his own territory. Probably because he relied on this, and the hostility which inevitably accrued towards the invading force, royalty-backed as it might be, he decided upon attack, not defence. And perhaps he overlooked that boggy patch at the foot of the hill. At any rate, the Gordons came down in hurtling force, and Huntly himself, with his banner-bearer leading, came to that soft ground. Their horses' hooves sank into the mire, and they stumbled. The earl's beast, all but collapsing, pitched the corpulent rider out of the saddle, to crash to the ground. And, soft as it was, there he lay, unmoving, although his steed struggled on and out.

Huntly was, in fact, dead. Heavy and elderly, his heart had made its own attack.

Mary and her ladies had been positioned on a small, flat-topped hill called Tornadearc, where they could view the scene from a safe distance. There they had dismounted, to watch, with a few guards.

They saw the section of Huntly's force detach itself, to head off eastwards to counter Atholl's people.

They could not perceive Huntly's personal disaster, of course. But they did see that the Gordons became in great disarray after that downwards charge, with their chief fallen and Atholl's and Morton's men coming at them in flank. The confusion extended to those left at the summit of Corrichie's hill, these uncertain whether to follow their colleagues downhill or to seek to combat the threat from the east.

The Lord James made an effective commander. He managed to win some order in the overall situation.

The Gordons accepted defeat.

It took a couple of days thereafter to reach decision. James, with Atholl and Morton and such other of the Privy Councillors as were available, ordered that Sir John Gordon must be executed for highest treason – the eldest brother, the Lord Gordon, having escaped. The prisoners should be taken to Aberdeen, for all the north was to be made aware of the price to be paid for treason.

There the captives and the enemy wounded were herded into the burial-ground of St Nicholas's Church. All the city's population was ordered to throng the streets, and the queen besought to present herself outside the provost's house, her half-brother James taking charge. He had a timber scaffold erected. Thither the second brother was brought.

Sir John, handsome head held high, leaped lightly from his horse, despite his bound arms. He inspected the heading-block on the platform, there before all, and turned to bow towards the queen, who was stationed to watch, however reluctantly. High treason had to be demonstrated as being against her, personally.

As the grim figure of the executioner mounted the scaffold, large axe over his shoulder, there was groaning and a stir from the crowd.

Sir John made a smiling flourish towards this newcomer, and turned again to face Queen Mary. He raised voice.

"Madam, your true lover stands here before you, at last. To say his farewell. I have loved, and sought to serve you well. I could have loved you even better, given opportunity. But . . . methinks you make but a cruel mistress!"

Mary, clutching a black crucifix, moved her lips but said nothing, her bosom heaving.

"You are the loveliest among women, madam; but your heart, I think, is of stone! I will embrace death now, as the warmer lover!"

John Gordon had certainly been a very attentive courtier.

"I have cared nothing for thrones and honours, Your Grace, these empty words," he went on. "It is for men – and women – that I care. But perhaps you are only a queen and no woman?"

The crowd was the more murmurous and restless.

James of Moray saw danger in this situation, for Aberdeen was very much in Gordon country. "Enough!" he jerked. He pointed to the executioner. "To your duty, man!"

"I salute Your Highness, and bid you adieu," the Gordon went on, seemingly unperturbed. "Who knows – perhaps we may meet elsewhere. Without benefit of so-called reformers!"

Mary swallowed, head lowered, eyes downcast, tears trickling.

The headsman tapped Sir John's shoulder, and pointed to the block.

The victim bowed again, and knelt to lay his head on the wood. Even there he turned his face to eye the queen, still smiling.

A shudder ran through the crowd.

The axe rose high, and fell.

The Lord James had to hold his half-sister up, as she swayed.

A second stroke ensured that the head was duly detached from the twitching body.

Weeping uncontrollably now, Mary fled into the provost's house to a bedchamber there. Save by her Marys, she was not seen again that day, nor the next.

She was thankful, two days later, to ride south.

The Lord Gordon was captured within the week, and taken to be confined in Dunbar Castle in Lothian, until parliament pronounced his doom also. But Mary interceded for him. The earldom was forfeited, but he was given release, so long as he left the realm. The same for his young brother Adam. That family had suffered sufficiently, she judged. As indeed had the Catholic cause.

Huntly's body was ritually disembowelled, and remained unburied until the parliamentary sentence of highest treason was passed.

So much for reigning over a united realm.

14

James Stewart, Earl of Moray and Mar, was now in fact ruling for his half-sister, she only *reigning*. Indeed he should have been king, she averred. Other monarchs, born bastards, had been legitimated by the Vatican. But Protestant Scotland would not accept that, and so was saddled with a female on the throne. As was England.

Mary was still hoping to contrive an interview with her fellow-queen. But the meeting-place remained a matter of contention, their advisers much at odds over it. Elizabeth's Cecil would not have her entering Scotland; and Moray and his like were equally against Mary going to York as she suggested. That was in Elizabeth's realm, and would not do. The suggestions as to alternative sites, the Isle of Man, Wales, or Ulster, were also ruled out, as under English domination. It looked to Mary as though France was the obvious answer. But England was permanently in a state of undeclared war with France, over Calais. And to go as far as the Netherlands or Denmark seemed absurd. The encounter remained in abeyance.

In all this, Mary was under constant pressure to remarry, and produce an heir to the throne. Various names were produced to her as suitable, none of which appealed: Don Carlos, heir to the Spanish throne; the Archduke Charles of Austria; even her late husband's younger brother, another Charles, now King of France, although that would require papal dispensation – not that she found him to her taste. Whoever it might be would become king-consort, which much limited the choice. Sadly her position did not allow her to seek out a man whom she could love and enjoy being wed to: that was not for a queen.

There was one young man at court whom it was suggested she might consider – and who certainly was apt to pay her attentions – and he was a Stewart, Henry, Lord Darnley, heir to the Earl of Lennox. Moreover he had royals links, for his mother had been the Lady Margaret Douglas, daughter of the Earl of Angus and Margaret Tudor, widow of James the Fourth, so he was her cousin. He was tall, well over six feet, which was quite important, for Mary herself was tall for a woman and apt to overtop many of her courtiers. And he was good-looking, with long fair hair but no beard, an almost feminine complexion and a ready smile. James did not approve of him, but others did, including Secretary Maitland and Archbishop Beaton. She could do worse, Mary agreed. And there would be no complications with other nationalities and royal houses, as there might well be if she was to wed the man whom Queen Elizabeth's ambassador, Sadler, was suggesting, Robert Dudley, Earl of Leicester, a favourite of the English monarch. It was sad that Sir John Gordon had had to die, for Mary thought that she might well have considered *him*.

Who would be a queen-regnant? Elizabeth seemed to enjoy being such, and, despite a glittering court, remained unwed, and with no heir other than herself, Mary.

There was a recent arrival at her court, with whom she quite quickly found herself on fairly close terms, but he was not of royal or even noble blood: an Italian named David Rizzio, who had come from Milan in the train of Moret, the Savoy envoy, a singer and musician, even something of a poet, a fascinating character who speedily established himself as an asset. He became Mary's valet; and when her French private secretary, Raulet, was dismissed for shameful behaviour, he was advanced to that position. Mary found him prepossessing and excellent company, although Darnly did not, nor for that matter did the Earl James and Maitland and others. But he, Rizzio, was a man with whom she could associate without any problems of rank or status.

Master John Knox found him an abhorrence, and said so in no uncertain voice, calling him a popish whoremonger and the queen his foolish gudgeon. He, Knox, had greatly gained in influence since he had won over the Scots parliament to endorse and adopt his Confession of Faith, a Calvinistic statement of no fewer than twenty-five articles stressing the presence of Christ in the Eucharist. Now, far from being merely a vehement minister of the capital's High Kirk of St Giles, he was the leading divine in all Protestant Scotland, and as such Mary and her advisers had to cope with him as best they could, even the Earl James walking warily where Knox was concerned – and that was becoming in matters more than merely religious.

This of Mary marrying and, hopefully, producing an heir to the throne was a constant theme of discussion at court. She came to the conclusion that it might as well be to Lord Darnley, who was obviously keen.

Plans were made for the wedding. Marriages were very much to the fore, for two of the queen's four Marys had just become wives, Mary Fleming marrying Secretary Maitland of Lethington and Mary Livingstone the son of the Lord Sempill. Dispensation for the royal one was necessary from the Vatican, since the couple were related; but Mary, presuming that this was forthcoming, saw no need to refuse Darnley's urgency. The wedding would be on 29 July 1565, a Sunday. One week before that, the groom was created Prince Henry and Duke of Albany. He was in his twentieth year, four years younger than the bride.

The great day dawned: indeed dawned was the word, for the ceremony was timed to take place at six in the morning in the Chapel Royal at Holyrood, this in order that the newly-weds could get to Falkland Palace in Fife, Mary's choice for that night. This entailed a long ride, thirty-five miles to Stirling to cross Forth, and another thirty-six eastwards thereafter. But Mary was a very good horsewoman and this would not tax her.

At the chapel it had to be a joint service, for Darnley had become a Protestant. Radiant, Mary, still wearing a black mantle over her white silk and jewellery, to indicate that she was a widow and formerly Queen of France, proceeded up the aisle, one hand on the arm of Lennox and the other of Argyll, this again to emphasise the dual religious backgrounds of the couple. The nuptials would be conducted jointly by Archbishop Beaton and the Reverend Robert Paterson, however opposed they might be towards each other.

Darnly, waiting at the chancel steps, was splendidly dressed and looked proudly handsome, already being referred to as Your Grace by attendants. He made a quite spectacular bridegroom, with his long legs, golden hair and confident bearing. For her part, Mary had never looked more queenly, as she kept comparing this with her previous wedding at Notre-Dame those years ago. The two bridegrooms could hardly have been more different. She noted thankfully that Master Knox was not among the clergy thronging the chancel. No doubt he would condemn this as but popish mummery.

The service was inevitably prolonged, since both faiths had to be duly represented. At the nuptial mass, Darnley knelt but did not partake, and was then given the Eucharist, Mary, head bowed, at his side. Most of the congregation undoubtedly were Protestant and the division was very evident. She wondered how their loving Creator saw it all.

The Abbot of Holyrood provided a sumptuous break-fast. Then it was time for the seventy-odd-mile ride, after Mary changed her garb. The queen's Marys were present, two now with husbands; but it was not considered suitable or apt that they should ride with the royal couple on this occasion. An escort of armed horsemen of the guard would come some way behind the queen and new king-consort. The lengthy journey might test even them. Mary's riding ability was legendary and, needless to say, Darnley was not to be beaten at it by a woman. Their mounts, to be sure, were of the best.

They spurred off up the Cowgate, heading for the West Port of the walled city, the streets thronged with cheering crowds, delaying them somewhat. Then it was out by the Haymarket and Corstorphine, on the road to Linlithgow, eighteen miles, and so on a similar distance to Stirling. Fortunately the weather was fine, although cloudy.

Darnley soon gave up endeavouring to show himself better in the saddle than his bride, and often Mary was in the lead.

Reaching Stirling, through the Tor Wood, in good time, once across the bridge they turned eastwards at Cambuskenneth Abbey, for Menstrie and Tillicoultry and Kinross. By then they were beginning to see, far ahead, the twin peaks of the Lomond Hills; at the foot of the eastern one lay Falkland. "Yonder, below the Lomonds, is our destination," Mary said, pointing. "The most favoured of all the houses I have inherited."

"Why name these mere hillocks Lomond?" she was asked. "The true Lomond is in my country, Lennox. Ben Lomond, three times as high as these."

"I am told that Lomond means a beacon, or place of beacons, the Gaelic being *laom*, the word for a blaze of fire in the old tongue. Do you know the Gaelic, Henry?"

He shrugged. "My father does. I had a sufficiency learning the French and the Spanish."

"Yet we Stewarts both have the ancient blood. Otherwise I would not occupy the throne. Or *we* now, to be sure."

"I prefer to esteem my French ancestry."

"French? Have you any such? *I* am half French, yes. But you?"

"The Stewarts were Normans."

"*They* were not French but Norsemen, Vikings. Does the name of Normandy not tell you that? Ralph, the Ganger as he was called, first Duke of Normandy, settled there from Norway. So we Stewarts are of Norse blood. A descendant, one Alan, son of Flaald, came over to England with William the Conqueror, and received the lands and castle of Oswestry in English Shropshire. He had a son, Walter, who came north to Scotland with the then King David the First's English wife, Matilda of Huntingdon. He founded a church in Glasgow. David made him his seneschal, or steward of the royal household, and so our name and style began. That, I think, was in the year 1204. Surely you must know of this?"

Henry of Darnley was less interested in ancestry than

was his new wife. "This Falkland we go to? Is it a fair house? A hunting-seat – but more than that? A dwelling of some comfort?"

"Would I be taking you there if it was not, Henry? It was built by my ancestor James the Third, and largely added to by my father and mother. It will be sufficiently comfortable, I assure you." Even to herself, it seemed strange for a queen to be vouching for the state of their destination to her new husband thus.

The keeper of the palace, who was also known as Ranger of the Lomonds, Royal Forester and Steward of Fife, had all prepared for them, late in the day as it now was.

Mary was not unaware of the speculations at the back of her mind as to what the immediate future held for her. She was all woman, and had been by her circumstances denied the full expression of her femininity, her previous marriage being no more than a gesture, a travesty of wedlock. Courtiers here, as in France, had not failed to demonstrate masculine attractions towards a young woman, and she had been fully conscious of such, but not in a position to respond in any evident way. Now she had an adult husband, and a good-looking and presumably eager one.

Darnley, however, appeared to be in no hurry to proceed upstairs to the three rooms prepared for them, lingering over the wine. No entertainment had been arranged on this special occasion, and for once they were unaccompanied by courtiers, or even the four Marys. Was it up to her to make the move?

Presently she laid aside her goblet, and rose. "Are you weary?" she asked, eyebrows raised. "With long riding?"

"No-o-o. But you may be?"

"Not greatly so. But perhaps . . ." She could not declare

that the bed beckoned on this their wedding night; nor that killing time was scarcely apt for the occasion. "I will go up now."

"Very well," he said, but did not rise.

In the bedchamber, with its great canopy-hung four-poster, Mary paused for a while. She then disrobed, to examine herself in the handsome Venetian mirror. Would he be satisfied? She was sufficiently shapely, she judged, long of leg, as was he, shoulders quite wide, neck also long, breasts full without being heavy, stomach nowise protruding. She knew her four Marys' bodies well enough to compare, and did not see herself as in any way inferior – and she was taller than them all.

She washed in the warm water provided.

Darnley seemed to be in no hurry to join her.

She asked herself what was in store for her. That must be quite normal wondering for a wedding night, although some young women would have rather more knowledge than had she, a queen from an early age and so not in any way experienced in the matter.

In a bed-robe she waited a while. Then deciding that this was ridiculous, she went to lie down on the bed. It was scarcely how she had visualised the situation.

Recumbent, she was anything but sleepy.

She had quite a lengthy wait before at last the door was opened and her bridegroom entered. He made no apology for delay, indeed he said nothing at all, undressing in careful fashion, more heedful of his fine garb than Mary had been for hers. Not troubling to wash, he came to the bed, naked, but in no way betraying evidence of eagerness. He got in beside her, but less than close, pulled up the covers, and lay on his back, wordless. He did not reach out to her.

Silent they lay.

It was not for the woman to make the first move. Darnley had always seemed interested in her, as more than just his liege-lady. Now he gave the impression of being almost detached, remote.

Mary did not actually count the minutes, but presently it dawned on her that, still on his back, her new husband was asleep.

Astonished, she wondered and wondered. Was he unmanly? Caring little for women? Married to her only that he might become king-consort? She had heard of such men, who preferred other men. Or was he merely not concerned with bodily satisfaction? Not that she was eager for his masculine attentions; but this seemed a very strange situation. What had she married?

Long she lay, listening to his deepening breathing. Would he wake presently, refreshed, feeling more active?

How long it was before sleep overcame herself, Mary Stewart knew not. Perhaps that regular sound of breath from her bed-mate eventually lulled her into the like state.

Some time during that strange night she wakened, but the man at her side did not. Whatever else, Henry, the new king-consort, was a good sleeper.

When, in the morning, the maids brought in hot water for ablutions, and Mary rose to wash, she saw that her husband was awake.

"You sleep soundly," she greeted him. "I wish you a good day, Henry."

"My thanks," he said. "And you." That was all.

Realising that he was watching her as she washed, the top half of her unclad, she judged that this had no effect on him. When he, in turn, rose to wash and shave, she observed that they had had an undisturbed night, this not exactly an accusation but quite a significant comment in the circumstances. Yawning, he nodded.

"You seemed to sleep well. After a full day."

"Yes. Blest be a bed!"

"Mmm. Even a shared one?"

"I make no complaints as to that."

"Was it . . . unusual for you?"

"Perhaps," he said. That man was not one for confidences, it seemed.

"Now that we are wed," Mary said, donning her bodice, "we will have to become used to . . . sharing much! As well as the crown! Even if we do not share in the Mass! You are strong for the reformers' cause, Henry?"

"I esteem it right."

"No doubt you do. On that we go our own ways, like so many others in this land. But we can be close otherwise, husband."

He did not comment on that.

Mary was wondering, indeed, how close they would get, with that man seeming far from urgent. She had had an inadequate first husband, the sad boy-king. Was this going to be little better? But give him time, she told herself. Strange that he had seemed more attentive to her before their marriage than now . . .

15

Darnley – for all thought of him as that, although he was now Duke of Albany and king-consort – remained anything but an attentive husband. He lived his own life, much of it in the streets of Edinburgh, associating with whom he would, not all respectable, with many suggesting that he was more interested in his fellow-men than in women. He had kept his own lodgings in the Cowgate, and much frequented them. Sometimes he accompanied Mary on her monarchial duties around the land, but by no means always.

One man, other than the Earl James and Maitland, who, perhaps inevitably was very much in her company was her private secretary David Rizzio. Lively and stimulating, he was never far from the queen's side, catering for her fondness for music, dancing and the like. Maitland, as Secretary of State, became somewhat resentful of the Italian's influence with the queen, so much so that James, her half-brother, warned her that this could have unfortunate consequences, arouse talk, and quite possibly incur her husband's enmity; she for her part suggesting that the duke was insufficiently interested in her personally, to care.

Whether this confidence got back to Darnley or not, one night thereafter, Mary in bed, at Wemyss Castle in Fife, visited from Falkland, he abruptly did what he had hitherto avoided. Waking her from sleep he quite violently forced himself upon her, and this without any preparation by love-play. To her pleas for care, gentleness and patience – for she was, of course, still a virgin – he heeded not, and in due course came to *his* physical satisfaction, if not to hers.

She rose, to wash, astonished and considerably agitated, and lay awake long thereafter as he slept.

And the following night, without any reference to the happening during the day, he repeated the assault – for that is what it amounted to – all so unexpected after the long period of seeming lack of interest in the like. He was her husband, but . . .

What accounted for this sudden change in his attitude and behaviour? The only possible clue she got was that he had decided that she was seeing too much of that secretary of hers, "the damnable Italian".

Mary sought to play the good wife as best she could, whatever her husband's shortcomings.

Unfortunately the arrival in Scotland of a newcomer did not help with regard to Darnley. This was the homecoming of the new Earl of Bothwell, James Hepburn. Mary had last seen him in France, where he had gone after his father's exile to England for various misdemeanours against the regency of Marie de Guise. She had liked the young man. Now his father had died, and he had come home. He had large lands in the Borderland, both in the East and West Marches, his mother being a daughter of a previous Lord Home.

It so happened that the present Lord Home had just died, and he had been Chief Warden of the Marches. His son was too young to be entrusted with such position. So Mary had Bothwell appointed, as seemed suitable, this to Darnley's opposition, who resented any favours being shown to men with whom she was friendly.

The Earl James came to his half-sister to inform her that

her husband had denounced Bothwell to the Lords of the Articles, of whom he, Moray, was one, declaring him to be in Queen Elizabeth's pay, and intent on forming a pro-English faction, as against pro-French, and naming that queen as heir to the Scottish throne, this based on the marriage of Mary's grandfather, James the Fourth, to Margaret Tudor. But such claim was hated and derided in the northern kingdom, as possibly leading to a union of the two nations, with England having ten times the population, and ever aggressive towards Scotland. Bothwell, of course, denied any such affiliation, but Darnley maintained his assertion, presumably out of jealousy. Mary was faced with rumblings at court and in parliament. But fortunately Mary was now pregnant.

She asked James what she was to do to put an end to these allegations and insinuations. She was advised that a public declaration from the throne that there was no possibility of a union between Scotland and England, and that even if Elizabeth died, and *she*, Mary, became monarch of both realms, it would be written, signed and sealed that the kingdoms remained entirely separate and independent. There was no English threat.

So a statement was made by the queen, this to the Lords of the Articles, to that effect. Her husband declared that this would put Bothwell in his place, the latter assuring all that he had no such mission, policy, nor instructions from Elizabeth nor her advisers.

Mary asked herself why she was plagued with these complications. And why had she ever agreed to marry Darnley?

However, in one respect, her pregnancy by him did commend itself to her. A child, male or female, would greatly improve the situation, as heir to the throne, and would please Darnley, proving his manliness.

That man proved, if not his masculinity, at least his capacity for drastic action. For, returning from one of his roisterings in the streets of Edinburgh to Holyrood, on the evening of 9 March 1566, with his associate Patrick, Lord Ruthven, and others he found Mary, now in her sixth month of pregnancy, having supper with the Countess of Argyll, the Archbishop Beaton and David Rizzio. Shouting his fury and accusations, he pointed at her to his companions, and these drew daggers. They seized the Italian and dragged him away from the queen, he grasping at Mary's skirts and crying on her to save him, save him! But too late. One of the conspirators, a Douglas, actually first stabbed the secretary over the queen's own shoulder, while Kerr of Fawdonside held a pistol to her breast. Thereafter no fewer than fifty-six stabbings were inflicted on the screaming victim, Darnley watching. Rizzio was left in a pool of blood, with the king-consort's own dagger still sticking in the body, as indication that he had sanctioned the slaying.

Devastated, appalled, and in fear for her own life, Mary was confined in her apartments while Darnley demonstrated that in this situation he was assuming full power. A state of emergency was announced, all Catholics in the city to be confined to their own houses, the Earl of Morton, the Chancellor, with his Douglases, to hold all the city in armed grip.

In the midst of this crisis, the Earl James, who had been in England, arrived home, and sought to aid his half-sister. He had a contempt for Darnley, and was backed by most of the powerful lords. He contrived Mary's escape from Darnley's clutches, not difficult, with her husband ever at his unseemly behaviour in the city's streets with Ruthven and others, and took her and her four Marys to Dunbar

Castle, down Forth, where Bothwell was acting keeper. In that all but impregnable stronghold, set on rock-stacks rising out of the sea, she was at least presumably secure.

It all made an extraordinary situation, the pregnant Queen of Scots cooped up in a comparatively minor fortalice while the king-consort ordered the rule, yet with most of the nobility and population against him. Clearly this could not long continue.

James and Bothwell laid their plans. The queen could, and should, call a parliament, whereat the will of the people was to be demonstrated. But that required forty days' notice, and by that time the child could be born, that all-important infant, heir to the throne. Darnley was only consort, a nominal position. If Mary should die in childbirth – and she had been having bouts of dizziness which the physicians shook heads over – then this infant would be the monarch, not the child's father; and parliament would have to appoint a regent to rule. Darnley was unpopular, and would be unlikely to be given the position. Who, then? The Hamilton Duke of Chatelherault was the nearest in line, legitimately, but he was a weakling and with no ability to govern a nation in turmoil. The Earl James was at least the late monarch's son, and Bothwell led in his support.

Darnley must not get hold of his child. How could it be assured of security? This Dunbar was strong, yes, but it was small, only a comparatively minor establishment. One of the great national citadels, Edinburgh, Stirling or Dumbarton Castles, should be the birthplace of this child. But Darnley's father, Lennox, was keeper of that last. Stirling was sixty miles away, Edinburgh only twenty-five. Its present keeper was Archibald Haldane of Gleneagles, a reliable man. Could Mary ride those miles safely in her present state?

She said that she could, so long as her horse went at a rate not to produce any premature labour. She would not hear of the use of a litter.

So next day the cautious ride commenced, and at a walking pace, Mary aided up into the saddle by her brother. By Prestonkirk and Haddington, the Gled's Muir and Tranent and Musselburgh they went, Mary apt to be biting her lip at the inevitable swaying and jerking. It made odd conditions for a monarch about to bear an heir.

They reached the Canongate Port safely, after about four hours. Darnley would be in the city somewhere, and they certainly did not want him to hear of their arrival and interfere. Mary had herself wrapped in a rough plaid; and her four Marys, with all knowing them, sent off by a different route by the Cowgate and Grassmarket, with the guard, while the queen, with James and Bothwell, headed straight for the castle, up the High Street and the Lawnmarket.

At the gatehouse above the tourney-ground, identity revealed, they were welcomed into the citadel on its precipitous rock-top by Haldane, and led to the palace quarters in a square tower near St Margaret's Chapel, on the highest point of all. The quarters here were not so fine as those at Stirling, but they were adequate, and at least with splendid views in every direction, north across the Forth to Fife, west to the Highland mountains, distant as they were, east to the Craig of Bass and the Isle of May, and south, less far, to the barrier of the Pentland Hills. This was to be Mary's residence for the critical and momentous weeks to come. None could reach her here without her agreement.

What of Darnley? He was known to be still in the city. If he desired to see his wife at the birth of his child he could scarcely be refused. Mary was contemplating divorce;

indeed, on James's advice had sent an envoy to Rome to seek papal agreement. But meantime he was still her husband.

It was now June. Calculations as to the day of birth were various, but within the first half of that month. The group of women around the queen were greatly exercised and concerned; indeed one, the Lady Reres, a believer in the occult and enchantment, not to call it witchcraft, offered to lie in bed near to the queen in order to relieve her of much of the pains of travail by personal substitution. Mary thanked her, but did not anticipate any relief from such generous overture.

As well that she did not, for she was not spared suffering. On the 15th of the month she developed pangs, which she assumed were the start of her delivery. But, no – nothing came of these. It was not until three nights later that they recommenced. And a grievous ordeal these heralded, with long and sore labour. It was not until the forenoon of the 19th that at last she was productive, and of a son, an apparently healthy infant although his legs seemed not exactly twisted but knock-kneed. All being well, Scotland had a future king.

Mary had decided to call a boy James, in the long line of Stewart monarchs, herself the only interruption – James the Sixth, but presently only Duke of Rothesay. She was thankful. She judged that she would not have to go through that ordeal again. She certainly was not going to bed with Henry Darnley; and even if the divorce was granted, did not see herself wedding another, however attentive were some of her courtiers, in especial Bothwell.

But she now had little James, and knew a sort of fulfil-ment. Congratulations poured in, including one from Elizabeth, although she was reported to have cried,

"Alack, the Queen of Scots is lighter of a bonny son and I am but of barren stock." Mary wondered at this phrase. How did the Tudor *know* that she was barren, unwed as she was? Or had she perhaps . . . ?

16

Bothwell acted with vigour to bring approximate peace and order to the unruly Borderland, as Chief Warden of the Marches, this territory, especially the West March, always a source of trouble and dispute with the English Borderers. He arrested a number of mosstrooping reivers from both sides of the line, and besought the queen to come and hold justice courts to try them, in person, this to confirm his authority and the need for harmony in this area. She agreed to go to Jedburgh, the county town of Roxburghshire, for this purpose.

She found the Borderland much to her taste, however riotous its inhabitants, the dales of Tweed, Teviot, Whiteadder, Blackadder, Kale and the rest in the shadow of the Cheviots highly attractive. But at Jedburgh, instead of Bothwell meeting her, she was informed that he had been attacked in Liddesdale in the West March by one of its trouble-makers whom he was seeking to arrest, a John Elliot of the Park, stabbed and severely wounded. He was now lying at Hermitage Castle, the Warden's seat on the Liddel Water.

Much concerned, Mary decided that she must go and visit him, she who had sent him to this task, lengthy ride as it would be and over very rough country, this with James and Maitland. She had been having those turns of dizziness again; but was not going to allow this to restrain her.

They went up Teviot to Hawick and into the hills south-westwards, by Bonchester and Southdean, a four-hour ride, from eight in the morning till noontide. Hermitage was a great and grim stronghold, as was necessary for anyone seeking to keep order in those wild parts. There they found the injured Warden being looked after by the motherly wife of the place's keeper, a woman quite used to coping with wounded men. Mary found her appointee recovering well, for Bothwell was a tough character. Assuring him of her good wishes she rode back to Jedburgh the same day, for she had another justice-eyres scheduled for the next October day, her companions shaking their heads over her all but feverish energy, for it made over a seventy-mile ride, and in misty weather and sodden moor-land. She even held a banquet in the town that evening.

Whether on account of this hard riding, or otherwise, her attacks of dizziness returned that night, and with grievous vomiting, her lady-in-waiting, the Countess of Argyll, counting no fewer than sixty spasms. Physicians were sent for.

There could be no more riding to Hermitage to see Bothwell. For a week Mary lay ill at Jedburgh, and many feared she would die, for any food she ate was promptly thrown up. All the realm got to hear of it, and prayers were said for her in all churches, Protestant as well as Catholic. She kept asking about her infant son at Edinburgh Castle. Many visited her bedside at Jedburgh – but not her husband Darnley.

Much talk of that man reached his sick wife. He was said to be plotting, with his associate Ruthven, to seize his little son James, have him crowned as monarch, deposing the queen, and he to rule Scotland as regent. Whatever the truth of this, he was a distinct menace to the peace and security of the nation; and Mary's advisers, led by her half-brother and Bothwell, decided that he must be dealt with. James advised banishment from the realm, but Bothwell advocated more drastic measures.

When Mary was well enough to ride the distance, she headed for the capital, and not for its great citadel nor for Holyrood but for the nearby castle of Craigmillar, belonging to the provost of the city, Sir Simon Preston, where she could stay, as it were anonymously; this because Darnley was known to be in the capital, and she wanted nothing to do with him. This latest folly of his was, in fact, nothing less than high treason.

Bothwell did not confide in the queen his plans for Darnley's discomfiture, however critical and concerned he was. But Mary learned of the consequences in due course.

Meanwhile there was the baptism of her son to attend to, he now almost six months old. It should take place at the traditional location, the Chapel Royal of Stirling Castle, this on the seventeenth day of December, as suitable before Christmastide.

It was a most notable occasion. Queen Elizabeth nominated the child her godson, and sent her Earl of Bedford, Puritan as he was, with a golden font for the ceremony, she recognising that this infant might well one day be King of England also. The King of France was represented by the Count de Brienne. The Archbishop of St Andrews conducted the service according to the Catholic ritual, and Jean, Countess of Argyll, another illegitimate child of James the Fifth, and therefore the boy's aunt, held him in her arms. It was noticed by all that Darnley did not attend. The Protestant lords did not actually enter the chapel, but stood outside, while the Catholic ones carried in the candle, the crucifix, the salt and the basin of water for the washing of the celebrant's fingers. As well that Master Knox was not present.

There followed much revelry, pageants, masques and entertainment with fireworks, Mary still less than well, but maintaining a cheerful presence.

But this attitude was changed by circumstances, dire events precluding it. Darnley had gone to his father's castle at Dumbarton and fallen ill there, some declared with the smallpox, others with syphilis. The queen, despite her own flagging health, had to show concern, for the man was still her husband, her desired divorce not yet sanctioned by the Vatican. He was king-consort and father of the little duke. She rode westwards, with her own physician. Darnley might be on his death-bed. Bothwell, for one, declared that this was to be hoped for.

At Dumbarton, she found the invalid partly recovered and announcing that he wanted to see his little son. Mary could not refuse this, and had a litter contrived, to be slung between two horses, for he was incapable of riding for any distance. The return journey was made, a curious situation considering the hopeless relationship between these two. The Earl James rode with them, but Bothwell would have nothing to do with Darnley, and kept apart.

The child had been left at Holyrood with the Ladies Argyll and Reres, and thither the father was taken. Mary, not desiring closer association, had him conducted to his own house in the city, at Kirk o' Field, near St Giles, Bothwell sourly having to escort him there.

Darnley clearly was not going to die of his malady, Bothwell decided and to get rid of him remained a priority. Means had to be found. Servants were sent to survey this house of Kirk o' Field.

It took a few days and nights to arrange. There were

cellars beneath the building, it was noted. Gunpowder?

Four nights later Kirk o' Field House was blown up and totally demolished. But Darnley's body was found lying outside it, and not grievously battered nor burned. He had been strangled. The word that circulated the city was that, as he was bed-going, he had heard sounds of disturbance going on below, and had gone down to investigate. He had found men carrying in sacks of powder, and, challenging them, had been assassinated.

Darnley had had many enemies, to be sure, but most believed Bothwell to be responsible, become close to the queen as he had. Was *she* involved, or in the know?

Mary Stewart was a widow for the second time, at the age of twenty-five.

The king-consort was buried at Holyrood Abbey, but Mary did not attend the Protestant funeral, preferring to perform any formal mourning that might be called for at Seton Castle, down Forth a dozen miles, the home of one of her Marys.

The Earl of Lennox accused Bothwell of his son's murder, but could prove nothing.

17

Mary had her worries, occasioned by more than the Darnley furore: the Catholic–Protestant controversy; the intrigues among her nobles; and that Elizabeth Tudor was blaming her, accusing failure to keep Bothwell in order, especially as Chief Warden of the Marches, claiming that he was positively stirring up troubles on the West March instead of keeping order there.

Mary's health was the concern. For some time she had been suffering from those attacks of dizziness, as well as vomiting, and she was now getting red patches on her skin, which were itching as well as impairing her good looks. Indeed, of all things, she began to fear that she had leprosy.

This was not so absurd a dread, in that Patrick, Lord Ruthven, had recently died in England of that disease, "the Finger of God" upon the victims, as this terrible scourge was called. And he and Darnley had been close, even apt to share beds on occasion. Could she, Mary, have contracted the plague from the father of her child? And might little James himself be harbouring it?

Mary was so concerned over this that she sent for one of her courtiers, Sir Thomas Kerr of Smailholm and Ferniehirst. He was a Knight of the Order of St Lazarus of Jerusalem, which specialised in the care and relief of lepers from crusading times when that dire ailment had become all too common among the Knights of the Cross fighting in those hot and outlandish parts. He was to go and enquire of experts in that order as to how to know the symptoms, and what treatment could be given if so it should be proved. Earl James and her other advisers, even her physicians, pooh-poohed the notion, but Mary remained anxious; and when two of the senior knights came and inspected her sores, declaring them mere rashes and nothing to worry over, she was not wholly reassured. Had she deserved such possible bane and punishment?

Bothwell was now very much in the queen's company, indeed some complained that he monopolised the royal attention. These were his enemies, who accused him of the murder of Darnley; although he declared, on oath, that if he could discover who made such false libels he would wash his hands in their blood. He was made keeper of Edinburgh Castle, in place of the Earl of Moray and Mar, her half-brother. In disgust at this James requested permission to depart the realm, and went to dwell meantime in Northumberland, this much upsetting Mary. How difficult it was to please all her friends and advisers.

The queen spent much time at Seton Castle, conveniently near to Edinburgh. And Bothwell, with all his various appointments and duties, found time to join her and the Marys there not infrequently. He announced that he was seeking divorce from his countess, Jean Gordon, a sister of Huntly, the reasons for which he left unsaid. She was a Catholic, of course, and he a Protestant. Mary's partiality towards him aroused much criticism among the faithful to her religion.

A parliament was held in April, at which Bothwell bore the crown and sceptre before the queen. And in the session thereafter he announced that Her Grace was willing to have abolished all laws that could affect her subjects in matters of faith. Also an act was passed providing for financial aid for poorer parishes and their ministers, this out of lands formerly belonging to the Catholic Church. Bothwell was in no way religiously inclined, but he could use the Protestant–Catholic division for his own purposes.

With the Earl James's departure to England, and with the parliament's consent the way was clear for Bothwell to demonstrate his ascendancy. On the evening that the session ended, he invited much of the nobility, although not the clergy, to a tavern in Edinburgh, and then surrounded the place with two hundred of his armed hagbutters. There he astonished all by announcing, now that he was divorced, that he had proposed marriage to Queen Mary, and that she had agreed to this, judging himself a suitable husband and guide. None there was in a position to contest this, however doubtful were some, especially those who believed that he was responsible for the death of her previous husband. Even those close to the queen wondered.

Presumably aware that there were questions as to the true position, Bothwell, ever concerned to express his views forcibly, devised a demonstration. On 20 April Mary rode to Stirling to visit her small son, lodged securely in that castle; and on her way back next day her party was intercepted at Cramond, six miles west of the city, by no fewer than six hundred horsemen under Bothwell; and despite the protests of his former brother-in-law, Huntly, Secretary Maitland and others, they were carried off far beyond Edinburgh to Dunbar Castle, of which Bothwell was still keeper, Mary not remonstrating like the others, this occasioning question as to whether she was privy to the entire proceedings.

At Dunbar, in the castle on its rock-stacks, the lordly ones were well enough treated but held secure, while Mary found herself conducted to a separate tower rising out of the waves and encircled by wheeling, screaming seabirds, on an upper floor of which she was allotted a bedchamber, in which she presently was joined by her captor. She was unaware that he had announced his intended marriage to her, and her agreement.

"I have long sought for this, woman dear," he asserted. "Just ourselves. None others to have to put up with. Always you have your attendants. But in this tower we are alone. How says Your Grace?"

Mary went to the window to look out at the sea and the seafowl. "What am I to say?" she asked. "You have me here, at your mercy! A woman, unable to protect herself!"

"And *would* you? Protect yourself, hold yourself aloof from me?"

"That depends, my lord. On what you seek."

"*You* is what and who I seek. All of you, Mary Stewart! I have wished for that for long. And have got rid of my Gordon wife. Aye, and you are a widow!" He came to stand beside her, a hand on her shoulder.

She did not shake him off, but nor did she turn to him. "You deem me . . . yours, do you?"

"I would have you so, yes. But you are my liege-lady. I must obey your royal commands. I have sworn, like others, to do so, have I not?"

"Must I command you to, to go hence?"

"I pray not. But you are the queen."

"You do not bring me here, I think, as queen, but as woman!"

"You are both. But it is the woman that I want." He all but shook her. "And you are . . . all woman. Beauteous and desirable: and kind."

"And you would have me kinder, no? And if not . . . ?"

"I judge that you would have royally dismissed me ere this if you were not . . . kind."

"So, it is my own fault? Is that it?"

"Fault? Or favour?" And his hand slipped down from shoulder to bosom. "Favour me, woman!"

"Have I any choice?" But she smiled as she turned to him.

James Hepburn required no further encouragement. He could not pick Mary up in his arms, for she was slightly taller than he, but he was strong enough to all but propel her over to the bed. There he threw her down, she scarcely protesting. And there he knelt, not in any supplication but to draw off her long riding-boots which she still wore, running eager hands up her silk-clad thighs as he did so. These stockings too he effectively pulled off. Then he rose, to grapple with her upper half – and to spare her fine clothing from over-urgent hands, she aided him in the loosening.

Her breasts, full and shapely, uncovered, he all but devoured them, pushing her back on the blankets the better to fondle and caress her. Soon his hands went lower, searching, exploring, before he stood back abruptly, to tear off his own garb, Mary watching and failing to cover herself.

As he had said, she was all woman. And neither Darnley nor young Francis had ever treated her like this. The essential female in her responded to his urgency.

Soon, both naked, they were joined together in passionate, almost fierce embrace, Mary knowing what she had never experienced before.

Bothwell might have his faults, but he was an expert and highly effective lover. He proved it that night, not once but many times.

18

Now, it was to be marriage, to be sure. Mary was well aware that most of her people believed that it was Bothwell who had had her previous husband, Darnley slain. So some demonstration as to his penitence, if not his innocence, was called for.

On 3 May a large contingent of his men, lances and swords for once deliberately cast aside, marched into Edinburgh from Dunbar. And behind them, on foot, came Bothwell, leading the queen on her horse, in a gesture of subservience and respect. Right up to the castle he led her, with its cannon booming out, and there made a show of leaving her in that secure place – although later he returned in disguise and was admitted secretly.

The wedding, Mary declared, would be celebrated on the 15th, at Holyrood. From the citadel she announced that her bridegroom was now created Duke of Orkney and Lord of Shetland, herself placing the ducal coronet on his head.

The nuptials, because of the opposition of much of the nobility and senior clergy, both Catholic and Protestant, were celebrated in a low key, indeed at the odd hour of four in the morning, in a mere chamber of the palace, Mary judiciously still wearing her mourning black scarf for Darnley. The Bishop of Orkney, not either of the arch-bishops, performed the ceremony, with Knox's deputy, the Reverend John Craig, and in his sermon included an announcement that the new duke repented of his former indiscretions and transgressions. There was no question but that the nation as a whole deplored this marriage. Thereafter there was no great banqueting nor pageantry, only a dinner in the palace for a few selected guests, this to make it clear that the queen had not forgotten the father of her child who would one day be king. Lord Herries, a prominent Borders magnate, had publicly implored her on his knees not to wed this dissolute man; and de Croc, the French ambassador, had also made it known that it was disapproved of by the Guise family and the French authorities in general – and, significantly, by her half-brother, James, Earl of Moray, who had just left that country for London.

All this caused Mary great concern and unhappiness. But she was committed, and believed that her union with Bothwell was for the best.

There was little delay in positive action. The great lords united to assert their disapproval, Argyll, Atholl, Morton, Angus, Glencairn, Eglinton and the rest. They put it about that Mary had been abducted and raped, certainly not accepting Bothwell willingly. They declared that the queen must be rescued from the clutches of this wretch. The Protestants were forming a confederacy, calling themselves the Lords of the Congregation, and vowing to rid the monarch of her new husband, by force if necessary.

Learning of this, and that his enemies were in possession of cannon to assail whichever of his castles he might take Mary to, Bothwell sought to counter this dire threat by using similar weaponry against them. The Lord Borthwick was Master of the Ordnance, keeper of the royal cannonry, and a loyal supporter of the queen. Moreover his castle of Borthwick was one of the strongest and least assailable in the land, set on an isolated hillock near Gorebridge, some dozen miles south of Edinburgh, and only a mile from one of Bothwell's own strongholds, Crichton Castle. He would take Mary there, rather than to Dunbar, which could be bombarded from the sea, and defy these trouble-makers.

They rode down into the valley that separated the two strongholds, to climb the other slope and over the ridge between. Each could be seen from the topmost tower of the other.

Across the Gore Water they came to Borthwick's dominantly grim tower, and perceived no signs of concern, the drawbridge lowered and no guards in evidence to challenge them. The sound of their horses' hooves did produce attention, however, this in the form of two youths issuing from the lofty E-shaped keep.

These knew their neighbour, Bothwell, of course, but not his companion. They greeted him warily.

"The Master of Borthwick and his cousin Will, Younger of Crookston," Mary was told. "Her Grace." That was abrupt. "Is my lord at home? Tell him."

Both youngsters stared at the naming of Her Grace, eyed each other, and then remembered to bow, bow low. Then they turned and hurried up to the first-floor entry, to cross the gangway to the keep.

The visitors dismounted.

The Lord Borthwick, a man of heavy build and middle years, hastily adjusting his garb, came wonderingly to greet the queen. They had met before, at court, but were not on any close terms.

Their host, needless to say, was much concerned over the news that the Lords of the Congregation were advancing in strength to assail Crichton; and if they learned that

Bothwell and Mary were now here at Borthwick, they would probably attack it in turn – and reportedly with cannon. Of all men, he knew well what cannon could effect against stone-walling at short range, as could be possible here. He was Master of the Ordnance to the monarch, but his duties were to supply artillery to the royal citadels, not to furnish his own castle with cannon.

"This hold will not stand against them if they bring their pieces here," he declared.

"It would take them time to get the guns here. Dragged by oxen to Crichton then across Tyne, over the ridge and across the Gore Water. The time that I need."

"Time to do what, James?" Mary asked, a worried young woman.

"To assemble my men at Dunbar. Get there, and have them back here to deal with these rebels."

"Then, we do not bide here?"

"*I* do not. You, Mary, must, meantime. Secure here. Until I return with my strength."

"But if they assail us with their cannon?" Borthwick demanded.

"Tell them that we are gone. The queen with me. Keep Her Grace hidden."

"But if they bombard? I cannot hold out against cannon."

"They will not if they believe us gone."

Unhappy, Borthwick was not convinced. But the queen's safety had to be his prime concern. And the rebels might not come to his castle, might not learn of Mary's presence here.

It was decided. Bothwell and a small escort would be off for Dunbar, a score of miles, to return in force. Mary to remain. It would take time, to be sure . . .

And time was not given them. Guards up on the battlements reported that there were horsemen on the ridge between the two valleys, watching. So they would see Bothwell spurring off. It would have to be by night, in the dark.

However, a thought occurred to Bothwell. If his escort of a few men were seen to leave, they would almost certainly be intercepted. They would declare to the enemy that their lord, and the queen, had already gone. To Dunbar. Hopefully they would then leave Borthwick alone, and head north-east for that castle on the coast.

Distinctly alarmed by this duty, five men were sent off, to be halted by the foe, and questioned undoubtedly, and to misinform.

When darkness fell, Bothwell took his leave, slipping out of the castle, alone, by a postern door. He would make for the small fortalice of Cakemuir, held by one of his own vassals, a Wauchope, three miles to the east. There get a horse to ride for Dunbar.

But he would be back, and not alone.

The enemy, in major force, had surrounded the castle, under Morton, Boyd and others, but so far without cannon, such, ever drawn by oxen, slow-moving indeed. No doubt they would appear in due course. And then?

Borthwick would have to parley with them, some of these lords being friends of his own. He would tell them that the new duke had gone. But the queen? If he said that she was still with him here, they would demand to see her, almost certainly hold her. Better to imply that she had gone with Bothwell. Hold out against the besiegers, at least until the cannon came. That might well be not before darkness, if they were coming, as was likely, from Edinburgh Castle.

Could the queen then slip out, as Bothwell had done, with guides, to take her under cover of night to Cakemuir, and thence to Dunbar? She agreed that this was probably best.

All waited for those cannon.

These had not come by nightfall, drawn on sleds, and covering no more than two miles in an hour, if that.

Once it was dark, it was time for Mary to move. The castle was as closely surrounded as the terrain allowed; and, not to be captured, the escapers would have to be cautious indeed. Fortunately the young master and his cousin were, of course, very familiar with the vicinity, and they had with them a friend, Sir Thomas Kerr of Smailholm, son of Ferniehirst, near Jedburgh, whom Mary had knighted the previous year. He would assist.

The queen could not depart by the normal exit, this because it was at first-floor level, from which a gangway was pushed out to reach a stone platform with steps down, a common security device. She would have to be lowered on a rope from one of the windows, a difficult and tricky performance for any woman, queen or other. But Mary was spirited and no shrinking female.

A long rope was produced and knots tied on it at intervals for the grip of hands and feet. Mary decided that this was not to be done in woman's garb; and borrowed some of young Crookston's clothing, he being tall like herself, even though this was scarcely made to fit her bosom.

They waited until midnight, when they judged that the besiegers would be at their least alert, including their torch-bearers. Then, choosing a window opening on to the inner recess of the E-shaped stronghold, and so in shadow from the torches, they waited.

When a pacing torch-bearer had passed, they quietly opened the wooden shutters of the lower part of the window, and paid out the rope, anchoring the other end of it to the leg of the massive hall-table. There was a drop of some twenty-five feet to the ground.

When they decided that all was clear, for the moment, Master Will went over first, he seeing it all as but a great adventure. Then his cousin. Sir Thomas went next, pausing once over the window-ledge to guide Mary's feet on the knots as she descended. Lord Borthwick handing her out over the sill, she began the dizzy-making climb down on the swaying rope. It was fortunate that she was slender and agile.

Steering her down, knot by knot, Thomas, very much aware of the stone's harshness against their hands, guided the royal ankles. As well that she was in male clothing.

At length Mary was safely at ground level, and a different variety of caution was called for. Those torches were none of them very close, since their bearers might be shot at by defenders, but they did add to the problem.

Keeping heedfully in the shadows, Mary and her companions crept round the keep's walling to a part of the courtyard where stabling and outbuildings provided some cover. The master led them across to a little postern door in the outer walling, inconspicuous but massively timbered and barred. He opened this, praying that it would not creak, and they passed through.

There was still the moat to negotiate, with the draw-bridge up and the portcullis lowered. The young men had not failed to think of this, and declared that they kept a small raft hidden nearby, from which on occasion they could leave the castle unannounced on their youthful ploys. That would get them over the water.

They edged round, at one stage having to go on hands and knees to avoid the torchlight. At the raft itself there were still problems, for it was made only to carry two, so the ferrying over had to be done by degrees, the passengers crouched low.

But at length all were over and faced with the next difficulty: how to get away from the castle vicinity unseen and then through the enemy lines. Again the Borthwicks' help was all-important. This postern led through to a track that went slantwise down into the ravine of a burn, a little tributary of the Gore water. They were able to reach this last unseen.

Thereafter they were led to climb out on to a sheep-dotted hillside among tussocky grass and gorse bushes. Stumbling a little over these until their eyes became adjusted to the gloom, they went carefully, not wanting those sheep to become too obviously disturbed.

Mary by no means held the men back. They saw no signs of the enemy up on the higher ground as they headed eastwards for Cakemuir.

Reaching that small castle, slow walking in the darkness over the rough terrain, they found Bothwell still there, in fact asleep on a bed, this seeming something of an anticlimax after their dramatic leaving of Borthwick. Wakened, Bothwell said that he had sent Wauchope to gather a sufficiency of men and horses to make the journey safely to Dunbar.

In the morning they rode by Fala and Keith, by the foothills of the Lammermuir Hills for the coast, Kerr leaving them to head south for Teviotdale.

Bothwell announced that Wauchope had told him that the confederate lords had summoned considerable reinforcements from the Merse and Borders area, Homes and Elliots and Turnbulls and the like. When all these were assembled they would have a major army at their disposal.

He would have to arouse the citizenry of Edinburgh, ever loyal to the queen, to gather in arms on the Burgh Muir. He would lead them, with his own manpower, against these rebels. Mary must come with him, to claim the support of all.

Making for the capital, with some two thousand men, they got as far as Seton, where the lord thereof informed that the Lords of the Congregation, learning that the queen and Bothwell had escaped from Borthwick, had abandoned their siege and headed off for Dalkeith, a Douglas town where Morton was strong. Knowing that Mary, if not Bothwell himself, was assured of the favour of the Edinburgh folk, they were avoiding the city. Bothwell, to take advantage of their loyalty, would join them and seek a confrontation.

At Seton Mary issued a royal proclamation against the rebels, whom she named traitors, and called for all leal subjects to rise in arms against them. She would join them, in person, with Bothwell, on the city's Burgh Muir. But she added that she was prepared to pardon the transgressors if they would renounce their treachery and swear ongoing loyalty.

So, turning inland to the higher ground, passing Tranent and Elphinstone, scouts ahead, they made for the capital. They would show who ruled in Scotland.

They did not get that far however. In the Carberry vicinity, some three miles south of Musselburgh, the scouts warned that the enemy lords had left Dalkeith and were not far off, advancing in this direction, not two miles away.

Faced with this situation, Bothwell had to make swift decision. The enemy were almost certainly in much greater force than he was. Yet to turn and flee, and with the queen, was not the answer. Carberry Hill, nearby, was a fairly prominent landmark and could provide a fair place to make a stand, its height giving him the advantage. Raise the royal standard there.

Carberry admittedly was no mountain, merely an isolated hill of modest altitude. But any force having to attack uphill was always handicapped. They moved over, to make the ascent.

From the higher ground they could see the enemy, and sufficiently clearly to recognise that they were indeed facing a greatly larger host, three or four times that of their own. And as Bothwell considered this, a proportion of his present company, not his own men but those of his allies, perceived and considered also – and came to the conclusion that, vastly outnumbered, they were in a very dangerous situation. They were not prepared to lay down their lives for the murderer of Darnley, whatever the queen judged. Hasty retirement therefore; and while Bothwell declared a stand on Carberry Hill their reluctance dictated otherwise. They were for off, call it desertion if that new duke would, and did.

So suddenly he was left with only a comparatively small number of men, there on the hill, and facing the nation's most experienced military commander, Kirkcaldy of Grange, with the confederate lords.

As they waited, uncertain, envoys under a white flag came spurring uphill to them. These announced that Kirkcaldy and the lords with him were entirely loyal to the Queen's Grace, and their quarrel with Bothwell only. He had to be delivered up. And they added that these lords had a second force round the back of the hill, to prevent any retirement thither.

Faced with this dire situation, Mary and Bothwell eyed each other, as well they might. It was a turning-point.

Although she did not know it, Mary Stewart was never to see James Hepburn again, not in this life, at least, whatever the next. And she believed that she was pregnant by him.

Abruptly that man turned, with a shake of his head but no words, and strode for his horse. Whatever his men were for, he was for off. Hoisting himself into the saddle, and with no further directions, intimations nor guidance for any, even Mary, he dug in his spurs and left them all there.

Astonished, bewildered, the queen stood, as the men around her began to melt away. Mary found herself left with only a handful of supporters. And they were surrounded.

In her sorry state she sent Cockburn of Ormiston to demand a parley with Kirkcaldy of Grange who had declared his loyal duty towards her, his monarch. He came, and she yielded herself into his hands – and hands it was, for he bowed to kiss hers, this before taking her horse's reins and leading it and her down to the other lords, some of whom were less chivalrous, including Morton, who shouted demands as to where Bothwell had flown. Dunbar? She could not say, she did not know.

Despite Kirkcaldy's assurances Mary found herself to be a prisoner. She was taken to Edinburgh, not to Holyrood but to Craigmillar Castle, Provost Preston's seat, he a brother-in-law of Secretary Maitland. There she was strictly guarded; so strictly that she was not allowed any women to attend her, and guards remained even in her bedchamber, so that she was unable to undress for the night. In despair and tears she laid herself down, a queen betrayed and deserted.

19

Next day, Mary was taken away, this in case the populace sought to rescue her. She was ridden no small distance, almost sixty miles, by Stirling and the Ochil foothills to Kinross on the shore of Loch Leven, and there confined in an island castle belonging to the Douglases, this in the charge of two lords who she much disliked, Ruthven and Lindsay. The owner of the castle, Sir William Douglas, was legitimate son of that mistress of the late King James the Fifth, the Lady Margaret Erskine; and she, a dominant old woman, mother of the Earl James of Moray, made Mary less than welcome.

Now the policy of the Lords of the Congregation was made known to the queen. She should abdicate in favour of her son, the one-year-old James, presently in Mar's care at Stirling Castle. Then she should retire to France.

She refused. She was Queen of Scots. An infant could not rule. Who then would? Chatelherault was a useless weakling, however close to the throne. She had a responsibility to the nation, and to her son.

Her captors threatened her physically. She was terrified. When she was told that the Earl James, her half-brother, could serve as regent for the child, she bit her lip, but still refused to sign the abdication paper. But when Ruthven gripped and twisted her shoulder, she gasped, and said yes, she would sign, if Moray, presently in France, came and assured her that the child would be well cared for and that *he* would act regent. But not until then. Meantime they could of course forge her agreement, but she would make it known that it was false, somehow.

They declared that they would send for Moray. But they would continue to hold her prisoner.

Meanwhile the coronation of the infant monarch would take place at Stirling, her eventual abdication being taken for granted.

Mary was in due course informed of the proceedings at the Chapel Royal. The Earl of Atholl bore the crown on its cushion; Morton carried the sceptre, Glencairn the sword of state; and Mar bore the child in his arms. John Knox preached the sermon, his usual thundering diatribe against Catholic idolatory, and the need for the boy to be brought up in the true reformed faith. The Archbishop of St Andrews, Primate, a Hamilton and brother of Chastelherault, refused to attend, so the crown had to be held above the small royal head by the only bishop who was prepared to do so in the circumstances, Adam of Orkney, this on the last day of July 1567.

At least Mary believed that her little son was well cared for at Stirling Castle by the keeper, the Earl of Mar. And now she was pregnant again.

The Earl James duly arrived back from France, and came to visit his half-sister at Loch Leven, unfortunately in the company of Morton, Atholl and Lindsay. He sympathised with her over her imprisonment, but said that he did not see how he could end it at this stage. He would accept the regency, and hoped that this might put him in a position to aid her better in the future. Meanwhile, he managed to whisper, at least he could help to control those confederate Protestant lords somewhat.

So Mary remained a captive, although once Ruthven and

Lindsay departed, she was nowise ill-treated. Indeed she became quite friendly with young Douglas, the castle's keeper, whatever the attitude of his grandmother. The son and nephew of Sir William, George and his cousin Will were quite smitten with the so good-looking captive, not much older than themselves.

Moray was proclaimed regent for King James at the Mercat Cross of Edinburgh, outside St Giles, Knox's church, the week after his return to Scotland.

Now that her small son had been crowned, Mary was unsure as to her own position. Was she still Queen of Scots? None other was; but in fact was she now only queen mother, no longer monarch? However, she had had no real power for long, so her title did not greatly matter, any more than when she had been Queen of France. Her situation was extraordinary, lacking all authority. As a queen she had scarcely been a success! Had she been a Protestant matters might have been different in this so-called reformed land. But she would cling to her faith, not fail in that, at least.

She underwent a major lift to her spirits, prisoner as she still was, when a few days later who should arrive at Loch Leven but her four Marys, sent by the father of one of them, Lord Seton, and the husband of another, Secretary Maitland. A third was now wed, Mary Beaton wife to Ogilvy of Boyne. But they remained devoted to their monarch and friend, and had come to tell her so. They were not permitted to remain with her, only to have a brief interview. She revealed to them that she was pregnant, although that was fairly obvious, this of course by Bothwell. And that she was being offered release if she would divorce her husband; this she refused to do, for it would make the child in her womb illegitimate in the eyes of Holy Church.

As to the new King James, with Moray as his regent, she declared that she would make his position more secure, when she had given birth, by retiring to France and entering a nunnery. Meanwhile she implored her ladies to prevail on their husbands and others to allow her to be held at Stirling, where she could be in the company of her little son, the king. Surely Moray would accede to this?

Her friends announced that they would do all possible to secure her relief, Mary Seton saying that her father would provide a sufficiency of men to protect her if she could get out of this island castle. The queen said that the young Douglases were inclined to favour her, and might well assist in an escape. The Marys agreed to speak with them and try to arrange it.

And then, possibly as a result of the stresses on her, she suffered a further blow. She miscarried and gave agonising premature birth to twins, both of whom died.

The queen wished that she had died with them.

Four unhappy days later, Will Douglas managed to see her alone. He said that if he could gain the key of the gate-house door, and believed that he might, he could have a small boat rowed in darkness thereto, conduct her down to it, and row her ashore to where Lord Seton would be waiting with an armed escort to take her whither she would. She was grateful indeed. She would be ready.

The next night it was contrived. Clad like a man, in riding garb, the queen waited until after midnight. Will Douglas came to her, declaring that all was ready. His cousin had got the key, and they had bribed the two gate-guards to feign sleep. The boat would be waiting, rowed to the gatehouse arch. He would take her down, and out, and with his cousin row her ashore.

She kissed him, in her gratitude, to his delight.

They crept downstairs and across the courtyard in the darkness. Under the arch they waited. Will had brought stones to cast, to make signals with their splashes in the water. This was not long in bringing the boat, with George and a servant rowing.

The supposedly sleeping guards above did nothing, and Mary was helped inboard, all going smoothly in as near silence as was possible, the oars wrapped with cloth at the rowlocks. Slowly, heedfully, they rowed well down the lochside for the shore.

Seton and his men were waiting there. Gratefully embracing the two young Douglases, and hoping that they could escape any punishment for their actions, the queen greeted her new rescuer, and mounted the horse provided. They reined round.

She was a captive no longer.

Dark as it was, they rode fast for the thirty miles to Queen Margaret's Ferry, where Seton had arranged for scows to take them and their mounts across Forth. Safely over, they continued to ride south west now the few miles to Niddry Castle, a Seton hold, quite a lengthy night-time journey. There they found the Lord Claud Hamilton, son of Chatelherault, awaiting them with fifty horsemen.

A few hours' rest, and they were off again, this time to Hamilton town itself, another thirty miles, where Mary's supporters were assembling.

She found large numbers awaiting her arrival, some she scarcely expected to see actively aiding her cause: the Earls of Argyll, Cassillis, Rothes, Eglinton, the Lords Somerville, Borthwick, Yester, Livingstone, Fleming and Herries among them. She was received with cheers. Between them they had mustered some six thousand men.

Who was the enemy? Strangely, it was Mary's own

half-brother, Moray, who as regent had to be seen to support the infant king, he with Kirkcaldy of Grange, and the still more fiercely Protestant lords.

The Lord Claud said that these were assembling on Glasgow's Burgh Muir; and he advised a move thither-wards to assail them before they had reached their full strength. This was agreed. And although Mary herself advocated parley, these lords of hers were otherwise minded. A blow struck now could be vital. Advance on Glasgow.

They got as far as Langside, just over two miles south-west of the city, and there were confronted by the regent's host. It seemed crazy, to be thus challenged by those marching in the name of Mary's own son, and under her half-brother Moray.

The Campbell, Argyll, who assumed the command, as Lieutenant of the Kingdom, was nevertheless insufficiently enough of a warrior to faint when faced with ordering the advance – although his partisans asserted that it was in fact an apoplectic fit. Whatever the reason, his leadership lacked brilliance, and he was faced by Kirkcaldy, the most experienced soldier in the kingdom, who directed the contest with his accustomed flair, although the Lord Claud, as commander of the vanguard of the queen's force, achieved an initial success. But this was quickly negated – and quickly was indeed the word, for the entire engage-ment lasted for less than forty-five minutes. There was, fortunately, no great loss of life on either side, Moray later claiming that only one of his soldiers fell, although the assessment was that three hundred of the queen's supporters were slain, this almost certainly an over-estimate in the cause of morale. At any rate, the efficiency of Kirkcaldy's command was emphasised by the long list of distinguished prisoners captured, these including the Earl of Ross and the Lord Seton, with the sheriffs of two counties, as well as Argyll himself, although Moray, in a judicious move, ordered his release, that he might abandon his allegiance to the queen.

Mary watched the brief battle from a nearby hillock. And as her people so speedily suffered defeat she cried out her distress and care for the losers, before, led by the Lords Herries, Fleming and Livingstone, she was reined away to leave the vicinity, to head southwards to escape capture.

Langside was one more sorrow to add to her long list.

20

John Maxwell, Lord Herries, took charge of the queen, an able man and a strong Catholic. Down to the West March with them, his own country, he Warden of that March. None of their enemies would seek to pit their strength against the mosstrooping Maxwells, Johnstones, Armstrongs, Jardines and Elliots. He could take Mary to his main seat of Terregles Castle, near Dumfries; but that might well be anticipated. Better to make for his smaller house of Corrah, on the edge of Galloway, among the fells of Criffell, wild and hilly country, a lengthy ride but offering best security until he could raise his Marchmen.

Mary was dejected. Fate appeared to be against her. She shook her head over Herries's project. No more fighting and deaths; enough blood had been shed in her cause. She would cross the borderline into England, making eventually for France. Elizabeth Tudor would aid her in this, if she could not find a ship to take her from some north of England port, Workington or Whitehaven or perhaps even Maryport, its name hopeful!

Herries, and even her four Marys, still with her, urged that she should not flee the land. The Langside defeat was grievous, but not in any way final. Much of Scotland could still rally to her standard, the Catholic north and the Highlands in especial. And Queen Elizabeth was not to be trusted, her Protestant leanings strong. She was Henry Tudor's daughter, after all, and could well see this situation as enabling her to get control of Scotland, the aim of England's monarchs since England was. France, if that had to be – but London never!

Mary was less concerned. Elizabeth was a fellow-queen. She would see that her, Mary's, position was not to be borne, and aid her, judge her recent imprisonment as shameful, and at least help her to get over to France. She would write to her. Meantime she would go to the Abbey of Dundrennan and wait for a reply. She should be safe there.

Her friends could not dissuade her. Herries, Fleming, Livingstone and the Lord Claud accompanied her to Dundrennan, a long ride, by Blantyre and Strathaven, Muirkirk and the River Urr. From that abbey, she sent a fishing-boat across the Solway to Carlisle, to Lord Scrope, the English Warden of the West March, Herries's opposite number, with a letter for Elizabeth, declaring that she was seeking her advice and requesting a safe-conduct down through England. Also she sent an especial token, a ring which bore the emblem of a heart, and which Elizabeth herself had given her years before. "Remember," she wrote, "I have kept my promise. I have sent you my heart in this ring; and now I have brought you both heart and body, to knit more firmly the tie that binds us together."

They waited at the abbey, which had so far survived the Reformation, well looked after by the abbot and monks. It all took time, of course. And, as the days passed, Mary grew anxious. The Lords of the Congregation would get word that she was here, and come for her, in strength. She must get away. Across the border, where she could be safe.

Her friends doubted the wisdom of this. Among Herries's mosstrooping clans she would not be endangered; whereas over in England, who knew what Elizabeth's minions might contrive. But those Protestant

Lords . . . ! There were Protestants across the border also, to be sure, but while she was awaiting Elizabeth's word and safe-conduct, she should be safe from these.

Nothing would do but that she must cross Solway into Cumberland. There would be horses to hire at one of the ports.

So it had to be parting for most of her supporters and friends, even three of the Marys. Only Mary Seton would remain with her, along with the Lords Herries, Fleming and Livingstone. A large fishing-coble was borrowed from the Dundrennan monks, farewells were said among some tears, and they cast off. From Workington, a score of miles across, Mary would send the word to Lord Scrope.

So the queen left her kingdom and her native land, to be rowed over to England.

At Workington Hall, the seat of the staunchly Catholic family of Curwen, known to Mary, she waited to hear from Lord Scrope. But he was now elderly and ailing, and his Deputy Warden, Richard Lowther, eventually sent Sir Francis Knollys with a letter from Elizabeth. He was to take charge of her and convey her southwards.

Herries, for one, said that since this Knollys brought no assurances from his monarch, no references to the heart-shaped ring token, only orders to escort the queen down through England, he advised caution. But Mary was not concerned. She would go and visit Elizabeth, and then on to France.

The final of the partings was there at Workington. Only Mary Seton remained with the queen to face the journey to London, with Knollys and his troopers. Kisses, more tears, heartfelt farewells and prayers for God's good protection.

Now Mary sent ahead of her, riding faster than could her company, the Lord Herries, to convey her letter to Elizabeth. Also the Lord Fleming, to go to France with a message that she intended to visit Catherine de Medici's court there.

So she proceeded southwards, in theory one queen on a sisterly call upon another while on a further journey; but in fact she all but a prisoner of Elizabeth's emissaries, Knollys and the Lady Scrope.

On their journey, one unexpected development much pleased Mary: her welcome all the way by the English Catholics, who seemed to see her as *their* representative as well as Scotland's. Indeed she was told that the Irish, fervent Catholics, were also looking on her to advance their cause.

She was not far on her way when, at Gosforth, she met one of Elizabeth's envoys coming north – not in fact to see her but to visit Moray – this a John Middlemore. He however informed her that her sister-queen could not personally greet her, this because Mary was being accused of being an accomplice in the murder of her husband, Darnley. Until such charge was proved false, there could be no actual meeting; but her good wishes were assured.

Mary was much upset by this reluctance of Elizabeth to see her, the more so in that Middlemore declared that Moray was to visit the English court and be welcomed there. This seeming duplicity on Elizabeth's part was worrying.

Knollys was proving to be no unkind captor. Indeed he gave the impression of being much aware of Mary's good looks, and appreciative. He declared that he was going to take her to Bolton, in the North Riding of Yorkshire, quite a long way off.

Riding thither they passed the first night at Lowther Castle, where presumably Richard Lowther, the English Deputy Warden of the Marches, had come from; and the second at Wharton. Just why they were going to Bolton was left unexplained.

But at that stronghold in Wensleydale she was pleased to find the Lord Herries who, having come from the court in London, was able to inform her of the situation.

Apparently there was to be a trial, *her* trial, this on Elizabeth's orders, on the pretext that she was being accused of being an accomplice in the murder of her husband, Darnley, in order that she might marry Bothwell. This travesty would find that she was innocent – this only however if she made declaration that she was advocating the abandonment of the Auld Alliance with France, and also agreed that her public attendance at Mass in Scotland was to cease, and the Book of Common Prayer be used in all Scottish churches. Once Mary was found to be inno- cent, she would be given assurance that she retained the Scottish throne, and the so-called trial would change into a conference, at which the Scots commissioners would be Moray the regent and Secretary Maitland, while the Howard Duke of Norfolk and others would represent England. The object of it all was to impose Protestantism more firmly on the northern kingdom. Mary herself was not to attend, any more than was Elizabeth. It was all devised by Cecil, the latter's wily chief minister, this in conjunction with Norfolk himself, the premier peer of England.

Mary waited at Bolton, with Herries, Livingstone, Boyd and the Bishop of Ross, Mary Seton and Lady Scrope in attendance.

In due course the queen learned that she had been found

not guilty at the trial, and was thereby accepted as still Queen of Scots – although all power in Scotland still rested with Moray as regent for her young son James, the monarch, now aged two years.

In the custody of Knollys, Mary was unsure as to what really was behind all this play-acting, while she remained a captive at Bolton Castle, contrived by the devious Cecil or perhaps the equally devious Elizabeth.

Knollys did not elaborate on it, but oddly that man was becoming quite attentive as to Mary's comfort and care, her looks and congenial nature clearly commending her to him. Indeed an extraordinary situation arose when he warned her against accepting the favours of the Duke of Norfolk, who was seeing much of her in the role of Elizabeth's principal representative. Feminine beauty could produce its complications on occasion.

Thereafter, much in Norfolk's company, Mary began to realise that he was seeking to convert her to Protestantism, odd as this seemed. The religious aspect of it he did not emphasise, if indeed that meant much to him; but the polity and governmental strategy side did. Apart altogether from Knollys's warnings, Mary became wary of this duke, recently become a widower. She recognised that he could possibly make a useful ally, but also that his attentions could become not only embarrassing but dangerous, if Elizabeth heard of them, which almost certainly she would.

"You, my lord Duke, are very kind to me," she said to him. "But might not your queen find that against her interests? I am here as her captive. And you are her foremost noble."

"And you are her heir, madam!"

"Mmm. And think you that would commend your kindness to me?"

"In representing her here, I would not have Your Majesty think *her* . . . unkind. The goodwill between the two nations must be fostered. There has been a sufficiency of enmity. I would see you as her sisterly guest, not her foe."

"That last I am not. But she favours my lord of Moray and the regency of my little son, not myself."

"*I* do not."

"Yet you represent her, at this meeting."

"In some measure, yes. But I also represent the best cause for England."

"And you judge that to be . . . ?"

"Peace. And a unity. And Your Majesty could represent both."

"I do not aspire to majesty, my lord. Only grace, as we have it in Scotland. Yet I am but a prisoner here."

"I would have it otherwise. You are Your Grace indeed, gracious, kind and fair. And a deal younger than Elizabeth. *She* will never marry. So one day you will be Queen of England as well as of Scotland. And formerly of France. The most queenly of women! Your lot here, in this Bolton, is disgraceful for Your Grace. I would see it bettered."

"How, my lord Duke?"

"I see you as wronged and maltreated by Elizabeth. But also by many of your lords. This Moray and his friends. You could turn the tables on them all, if you would."

"How so? In my state!"

"You could wed me!"

Mary stared. "Wed! Me?"

"Indeed yes. If we married all would be changed. You no longer a captive. Elizabeth baulked. The kingdoms could look forward to unity, not only an end to rivalry and warfare. She has no heir but you."

And you king-consort, Mary thought, but did not say so.

"I am Catholic and you are Protestant," was what she declared.

"That is no matter. We can worship as we will. I could make you a good husband, Mary. And win you out of Elizabeth Tudor's grasp. I have many castles and manors, and many friends. You would be a deal better wed to me than you were with those others, the boy King of France, that Lord Darnley, and the Earl of Bothwell, something of a rogue!"

She eyed him wonderingly, thoughtfully. He was a big man, not handsome but nowise ugly, square of features with a commanding bearing. Ought she to be considering this in her present position? She perhaps required a husband. And the premier duke and Earl Marshal of England could be as good as any she was likely to get. She would no longer be Elizabeth's prisoner, and difficult for that queen to counter. Give her an advantage as against her half-brother Moray, and even the Protestant Lords of the Congregation, if her new husband was a Protestant.

These thoughts rushed through Mary's mind as she temporised. "You . . . overwhelm me with your proposals, my lord," she said. "I am not in a state to consider all, here and now."

"Your state could be much bettered as my wife," he repeated. "You must see that. Have you aught against me as a man? My late wife, Elizabeth, who died a year ago, found no fault. Nor she whom I wed before, Margaret Audley, mother of my son, Arundel. They both found me . . . caring."

"I do not question that. But I require time."

"Take time indeed, Mary. And I will hope and pray for your good decision. I believe that I can serve you well in all. In hope, to your good pleasure. And mine."

169

He bowed out of the room.

Mary considered indeed. Was this the answer, *the* answer . . . ?

However, there came more to consider, and promptly, there at Bolton. Moray sent word that there had come into his possession certain papers, what became known as the Casket Letters, because they had been contained in a silver casket. These were written in French, and Mary always averred that they were forgeries. They allegedly revealed her knowledge of Bothwell's plot to blow up Darnley at Kirk o' Field, and her approval of the murder. Presumably Bothwell had had these written, in a feminine hand, to justify his action; and they made Mary an accomplice in the death of her then husband. Bothwell was now overseas, if he was still alive; and these letters could be used as a damning indictment. Now, somehow, they were in the regent's hands.

She told Norfolk of this, and that they were false. He declared that this was all the more reason that she should wed him, as further needing his protection.

But still she hesitated. Wed again? Her marriages had been disastrous. Would this prove any better, however advantageous it might be in some respects? She liked Norfolk, yes – but would being wife to the Earl Marshal of Elizabeth's England be advisable? Protestant as he was, and however tempting as a means of getting out of this captivity at Bolton?

After three days Norfolk brought her the decision reached by the trial-conference, this now being adjourned and transferred from York to London, so that its findings could be reported to Elizabeth and her reactions heard. The conclusions were these. Mary should ratify and renew her abdication, made at Loch Leven. She should remain in

England as captive-guest of her sister-queen. Elizabeth would provide revenues suitable to preserve her royal dignity; and she would be permitted to move her lodgings here and there, this under the control of himself, Norfolk.

So she was clearly going to see much of the duke, who obviously had so contrived it. Was that to be her future now, her fate? It could, she supposed, be worse.

21

This of the conference being transferred to London meant that Norfolk had to go with it – but not Mary. So new quarters had to be found for her, the duke considering Bolton too severe. He therefore arranged that she should be entertained, as he put it, at the houses of various of his friends, but keeping her well away from London. He would get back to see her as often as possible.

Thereafter she was moved from one castle or manor to another over a wide area of the Midlands, sometimes treated warily as Norfolk's friend but not Elizabeth's. She found Wingfield pleasant enough, but not Tutbury Castle in Staffordshire, a seat of the Earl of Huntingdon, whom she much disliked. It was a comfort to have Mary Seton with her. She often wondered how her other three Marys fared.

Then there was a development which further endangered Mary's situation and increased Elizabeth's displeasure. The Catholic Earls of Northumberland and Westmorland rose in arms, to seek to make the north of England a Romish enclave; and of course Mary, as the Catholic heir to the English throne, was considered to be privy to it all, if not actually inspiring it. She was promptly removed south to Coventry, to be out of reach of the rebels, and Norfolk, Protestant as he was, confined in the Tower, as possibly involved. Mary, more strictly watched than ever, was devastated at this imprisonment of her friend. She sent him an embroidered cushion, embroidery being how she passed much of her time, but he was never allowed to receive it.

The rising of the Catholic earls in the north came to nothing, and they fled to Ireland.

Mary was at Coventry when the news of the death of her half-brother, Moray, reached her. He had been gunned down in the High Street of the town of Linlithgow, by a Hamilton. Whether this had anything to do with Chatelherault was not known, although fingers were pointed, for it was suggested that he, or rather his more ambitious son, the Earl of Arran, sought the regency, as next in line for the throne. However, a hasty meeting of the Privy Council appointed the Earl of Lennox to that position, this to be confirmed by parliament; after all, he was the boy-king's grandsire, father of the late Darnley, although how strong a ruler he would make was another matter.

Nothing of this affected Mary's situation however, save that she was worried that Lennox might yield to Elizabeth's new suggestion that little James, now in his fourth year, should be sent to her care, as eventual heir to the throne of England, and educated there.

Mary was becoming used to being a prisoner and being ordered about by others, all but forgetting that she was a queen, at least in name. How had Elizabeth survived as monarch? And Catherine de Medici? And the late Isabella of Spain? Was she, Mary, just weak? Ineffective? Or was it because she was a Catholic in a mainly Protestant country, as she often feared? Was it her looks that were at fault? She well realised that she was good-looking, and that she attracted men, not always of the right sort – and she was not averse to the other sex's appreciation. Elizabeth and the Medici were not thus troubled. Were they fortunate in this as monarchs? Was comeliness of features and form a handicap when it came to ruling?

She was thankful to hear that little James was now entrusted by parliament to the care of the Erskine Earl of Mar, in Stirling Castle. He ought to be secure there from Elizabeth's schemings; and these were very much to be considered, for she had promised pensions for certain Scots lords to do her bidding, these including the powerful Douglas, Earl of Morton.

Norfolk arrived at Coventry from London to Mary's side again, although he confessed to her that he had promised Elizabeth to forsake all intercourse with the Scots queen, this in order to be freed.

"God forgive me for breaking my solemn word," he told her. "But somehow I had to get back to you, Mary, you firmly in my heart! If we wed, it would greatly improve your situation, my dear one. You must see that."

Eyeing him in his eagerness, she shook her head, almost reluctantly. "I am not ready for marriage, Thomas," she said. "Bear with me. I like and esteem you well. But marriage – not yet. A captive and exiled from my own land, hated by Elizabeth Tudor, I am in no position to consider it."

"Yet wed to me, the Earl Marshal of England, you could cease to be a captive. As Duchess of Norfolk, Elizabeth would have to accept you."

"Yet she put *you* in the Tower of London!"

"But had to release me, for fear of the realm's anger. I am its premier duke."

"How would your realm see you if you married the Catholic Queen of Scots?"

"Most would see it as good, as I told you before. Linking the two kingdoms in amity."

"Not most Scots, perhaps! Their little king's mother wed

to an English duke. With Elizabeth seeking to get my son into her clutches."

"I would see that she did not."

"Let us remain friends meantime, Thomas."

"As you will. But I will seek to gain support from all Catholics, Protestant as I am, for your release. And even bring in aid from France and Spain."

Soon thereafter, in that spring of 1570, Mary was again transferred, this time to Sheffield Castle, the policy obviously being to keep moving her, so that plots for her release by Catholic sympathisers might be frustrated. And such plots there were, a notable one conceived by a wealthy Italian banker named Ridolfi, in conjunction with the Duke of Alva, backed by King Philip of Spain. This was to invade England from the Netherlands with a large army, to coincide with a rising of the English Catholics, and in the confusion created seize Elizabeth at Hatfield Hall, which she much favoured, and free Mary. Wedding to Norfolk to follow, and the ascent of the English throne, much money being contributed from Spain and France to finance the enterprise and bribe supporters, this man Ridolfi, who was owed large sums by the continental monarchs, the brain behind it all.

Mary, at Sheffield, knew nothing of it all until, in October, who should come to visit her but William Cecil himself, Elizabeth's powerful Secretary of State, and Sir Walter Mildmay, to tell her that Queen Elizabeth was aware of the plot, and was demanding that she, Mary, publicly disassociate herself from it on pain of the direst consequences. But if she agreed to form an alliance with Elizabeth against the Catholic lords, she would be allowed to return to Scotland – but this with her son James delivered as a hostage.

Mary indignantly refused any such use of her small offspring, but pleaded nevertheless to be allowed to go and visit him at Stirling, promising a return to Elizabeth's keeping thereafter. And even Cecil was so much affected by the queenly captive's beauty and persuasive ability that he agreed to endeavour to bring her personally into Elizabeth's presence, so that their differences might be eliminated and a working relationship established.

Mary was hopeful.

But it was not to be. To prove the Tudor's unyielding enmity, Norfolk was promptly re-arrested and put back into the Tower. And Cecil, left in no doubts as to his folly, was ordered to convince the new Scots regent, Mar, to have Secretary Maitland arrested as advocating the marriage of Mary and the duke. This Mar refused to do, for he and the secretary were friendly. Shortly thereafter Mar suddenly died, not without suspicion of poison. The Douglas Earl of Morton, approved of by Elizabeth, was appointed regent in his place.

That unfortunate queen was now removed to Chatsworth House, in Derbyshire, the seat of Sir William Cavendish, where her gaoler proved to be the formidable, or notorious, Lady Cavendish, known as Bess of Hardwicke, who had had numerous husbands and mastered them all.

Mary got on quite well with this Bess, a large and hearty woman, who was fond of hunting deer as well as men, and took the queen with her on her expeditions, a sport which the latter had not enjoyed for long. Elizabeth's approval of this was unlikely.

It was while at Chatsworth that Mary learned sad news indeed. Norfolk was dead, executed on Elizabeth's orders for high treason, the allegation being that he had conspired to have her deposed, and to marry Mary as her lawful successor.

Tears flowed. Was she, Mary, doomed to bring sorrow and suffering on others as well as herself? Mary Seton comforted her, but Bess of Hardwicke told her not to be a fool, that Norfolk had all but asked for it. He had had a fair trial – her own husband, now created Earl of Shrewsbury, was one of the judges – and his declared intentions to wed Mary the height of folly.

Despite this, Chatsworth proved to be the most congenial of Mary's many prisons, where she felt least of a captive. In her present husband's absence in London this Bess, although twenty years older than herself, was quite the best "captor" she ever had, little as they seemed to have in common. And the queen's poor health, a constant pain in her side, agonising at times, had Bess concocting remedies from plants and herbs.

More news reached Chatsworth, and was retailed to Mary, affecting her greatly. There had been a most terrible massacre of French Protestants that August, and it had been led by Mary's kinsmen, the Guises. Starting in Paris, it had spread throughout France. Some five hundred of the higher-born Huguenots, as they were known, had been slain, together with as many as ten thousand of the common folk, this on St Bartholomew's Eve and Day, and in the name of the loving Christ's religion. This appalling tragedy, as well as utterly devastating Mary, resulted in herself, as representing the Catholic cause in England and Scotland, being execrated, with demands made for her death, utterly deploring it as she did. What had caused her uncles to advocate this atrocity? And Queen Catherine de Medici, regent for her young son Henry the Third? She had, after all, sought to reconcile the religious differences in France for years, yet now she appeared to have accepted the enormity of it.

Bess of Hardwicke asked if the French had run mad. Could Mary explain, or justify the behaviour of her kinsmen?

Then, shortly thereafter, came word that John Knox had died. He had been a sick man for some time, and indeed had ordered an especial coffin to be made. But he had maintained his Protestant evangelistic crusade until his last breath, and then raised a shaking hand in blessing on those at his bedside – non-Catholics, needless to say.

The Douglas Earl of Morton had succeeded the late Mar as regent, a much more violent and unscrupulous man, sufficiently so to petition Elizabeth to have Mary put to death in the cause of religion, this although he now ruled Scotland in the name of her small son. Large Bess told of this. She judged that *her* monarch would not concur in the execution of a fellow-queen. Sometimes Mary rather wished that she could move, or be moved, on to the next life, in which she had fullest faith, having had enough of captivity and the pains which these days beset her.

Bess told her not to be foolish. She was, after all, aged only thirty-one years, Elizabeth almost ten years older. And on the Tudor's death, *she* would heir the English crown, and her life would be transformed. Be patient! If Elizabeth had wed and had a lawful heir, it would have been different.

The Countess Bess was good for Mary.

The next news she learned was of a French plot to bribe the governors of young King James, even Morton himself, with sufficiently large amounts of money to allow the boy to be taken secretly away to France, this largely with funds provided by the Vatican. Whether the regent and the other lords would be persuaded to agree to this remained to be seen; but undoubtedly Elizabeth would seek by every means in her power to prevent it.

She did. When relevant tidings reached Chatsworth it was to the effect that a large English army had marched north to Edinburgh, under Sir William Drury, marshal of the northern forces and governor of Berwick, and had besieged the capital's citadel, bombarding it with no fewer than three thousand cannonballs before it had yielded. Secretary Maitland had committed suicide, by swallowing poison, rather than disgrace himself by surrendering the hold; and Kirkcaldy of Grange and his brother Sir James had been captured and executed.

Mary was utterly dismayed by this further disaster to her cause, especially the death of Maitland, her own Mary Fleming's husband and her so loyal adherent. As well as his fate, others of Mary's friends were captured, these including the Lord Home, Sir Robert Melville, the kingdom's foremost diplomat and envoy, and the Bishop of Dunkeld.

There seemed to be no end to her distresses and misfortunes. For it was reported that the long-standing alliance between Scotland and France, her second homeland, had broken down to some extent, this because Catherine de Medici had entered into a defensive compact with Elizabeth, being called the Treaty of Blois, and was proposing that her son, the Duke of Alençon, should marry the Tudor – although whether the hitherto determinedly unwed queen would actually commit herself to this was questionable.

Mary had reason to thank Bess of Hardwicke for much, not least for introducing her to Buxton. This was a Derbyshire spa, the highest market-town in all England, in the Peak District. As a bathing-place it had been famed even in Roman times, its mineral waters renowned for their healing qualities, not only with regard to gout and rheumatics but for female afflictions. Bess suggested that Mary's side-pains might well benefit from immersion therein as well as being drunk. It was near Chatsworth, indeed the land belonged to the Earl of Shrewsbury, and Bess made considerable profits from charging visitors for the use of it, as much as three pounds for a duke and lessening to twelve pence for common folk. There had always been a St Anne's chapel there, where the Mass was permitted to be conducted for Catholics in thanksgiving, also at a charge, which further commended itself to Mary.

The bathing procedure was simplicity itself. There were two ponds, near where the River Wye plunged underground in a waterfall, these side by side, supposedly for men and women, although the men frequently transferred themselves to the other pool, Bess's servants shutting their eyes to this, nakedness considered quite acceptable in this pursuit of health. And, to be sure, there was no discrimination as to rank, so long as payment was made, nudity scarcely providing evidence thereof. Mary had a highly attractive body, and did not object to revealing it in such circumstances. And larger Bess had no qualms either, although her size, masterful carriage and demeanour did tend to inhibit some masculine attention. Not so with Mary, and the pair of them drew considerable attention from all, especially the other sex. It had to be a custom and activity confined to the warmer months, of course; but so long as the prevailing temperature was not off-putting, clothing also got off-put, and a happy, carefree and beguiling freedom was apt to be generated, this acceptable to the captive.

So Mary found Buxton much to her taste, and Bess herself nowise reluctant, and her husband, when his court duties permitted it, likewise appreciative, this so much so that Bess asserted that she would have to watch her George heedfully lest he made off with the captive.

Another man who paid quite frequent attentions to Mary was the Earl of Essex, a favourite of Elizabeth's. It so happened that Chartley, one of his seats, was near Buxton; and although Elizabeth herself did not come to disport herself at the waters, *he* frequently did, and tended to gravitate into Mary's company. She found him amiable as well as handsome. Bess warned her to keep him at a distance as far as she could, for if Elizabeth heard of this, as no doubt she would, she would be displeased. And the Tudor's displeasure was not lightly to be aroused.

Mary found many excuses to visit Buxton, its Catholic chapel a valid one. And Bess, her guardian, observed that her body, hitherto white, was becoming quite brown with the sun, that summer of 1573. As captivities went, this was surely one of the least objectionable. Mary Seton, her faithful companion, enjoyed it all less, her skin being apt to blotch with sunburn.

Actually Elizabeth was presently at Chartley, hence Essex's attendance. But she, the Tudor, so strongly Protestant, did not approve of the Catholic chapel, and this of alleged faith-healing, so she did not visit Buxton. The two queens were quite physically near each other, however far apart in other matters. They did not meet.

Mary did meet Cecil, however, the Lord Burghley, the most powerful figure in all England after his monarch, his son, Sir William, confessing that Elizabeth was somewhat worried that Mary's charms and looks might be endearing to her courtiers, even possibly his own father. If so, the

Secretary of State was careful not to demonstrate it obviously. In fact young Cecil informed that his father had ordered Shrewsbury to keep the royal captive more "straitly" as he put it, presumably on Elizabeth's command. If that earl did not, in consequence, treat Mary much more strictly, no doubt as well as being affected like so many others by her beauty, he was remembering that when his present monarch was to die, the said younger and fairer female would become in turn his own queen. This recognition was apt to be at the back of many minds.

In these circumstances many of the great and noble families of the Midland counties did act kindly towards Bess's royal prisoner.

Unfortunately this pleasant interlude came to an abrupt end, this on account of Mary's well-wishers, or some of them. Anthony Babington, a young and staunch Catholic squire, concocted a plot, however impracticable. He and his friends sought the King of Spain's help. A Spanish fleet was to threaten the southern English ports, even to enter the Thames, this while he arranged the assassination of Queen Elizabeth. He would inform Queen Mary of his intentions, and foster a Catholic rising.

This he rather foolishly did, by sending numerous letters to magnates of the faith nationwide. Almost inevitably some of these were intercepted and conveyed to Cecil, including one to Mary. The rash young man was promptly arrested, with his coadjutor, one Ballard; and both were executed for high treason.

Although Mary personally was nowise involved in this hare-brained venture, she was assumed to be. And in consequence removed from Bess of Hardwicke's kindly care and transferred to Tixall, a castle of Sir Walter Ashton. Here presently Sir Amyas Paulet, one of

Elizabeth's close courtiers and a stern Protestant, took over, and carried Mary back to Chartley, a stronger hold.

Mary's previous stay there, with her friendly behaviour towards all and sundry, even her captors, had made her popular locally, however, and it was deemed wise, after a few days, to remove her out of that area. Paulet chose the castle of Fotheringhay, in Northamptonshire, a stern stronghold where he judged she would be secure from any Catholic conspiracies, such as that of the late Babington.

On the way northwards she spent two nights in the town of Leicester, in a house of the Earl of Huntingdon. And there the citizens surrounded the premises, cheering her and demonstrating their favour, these probably mainly Catholics. This alarmed Paulet; indeed his own coach had to be guarded from attack, while he sent for more armed men to increase his escort.

Mary behaved with her customary amiability towards this Paulet, but received no kindly reaction from that man, which was unusual – probably why he had been selected to be her gaoler.

From the hill shires of Derby and Leicester they came down to the lower ground around Peterborough, nearing the Fen country, where Fotheringhay Castle rose on its isolated mound, as stern and unyielding as was Paulet himself, this on the sluggish River Nene, with its double moats. The hold was bare and empty, with no comforts, and the queen, with Mary Seton and her lesser female attendants, eyed it unfavourably and wondered why they had been brought here, hoping for no lengthy stay.

Paulet left them then, under strong guard, not indicating why they were there, this on 25 September.

They made the best of it.

It was the first day of October before Paulet returned.

He announced that he had his orders. Mary Stewart was to be punished for her shameful involvement in the Babington Plot. He advised her to confess, as a most heinous sinner against his Queen's Majesty.

Mary shook her lovely head. "As a sinner I am truly conscious of my many offences against my Creator," she declared. "And I beseech his forgiveness. But as queen and sovereign, I am aware of no fault nor offence for which I have to render account to anyone here below. As, therefore, I could not offend, I do not wish pardon from anyone living."

Paulet duly conveyed this announcement to Elizabeth.

As a result, an especial commission was set up to examine, and to try Mary on a charge of treason against the Queen of England, for an involvement in the conspiracy of Babington to murder her.

This was held, on 15 October, in Fotheringhay Castle, however bare and unsuitable for such lofty company, for in judgment were the highest of Elizabeth's advisers: the Lord Chancellor Sir Thomas Bromley; the Lord High Treasurer Cecil, Lord Burghley; the two Chief Justices of the Realm, and the statesmen Walsingham, Hatton and Sadler. Also the Earl of Shrewsbury, who sought excuse from being involved but was refused, on Elizabeth's orders, as having, with his Countess Bess, treated Mary much too leniently at Chatsworth.

Before these, Mary was brought, and alone.

Eyeing them all, she shook her head, and said, "I see that my accusers do not lack counsellors. But *I*, I am allowed no counsellor. So I am condemned before we start, no?"

There was no answer to that.

She went on, "I demand to know why it is claimed that I am subject to this trial and to the laws of England. I came to this kingdom on Queen Elizabeth's advice and request, and to her protection. But I am Queen of Scots, monarch of an independent nation."

The Lord Chancellor Bromley took charge. "Her Majesty Queen Elizabeth has been reliably informed that this Queen of Scots has planned her fall, and indeed death. And this assembly has the duty of discovering whether this is true or false. I call upon Her Majesty's Royal Sergeant Gawdy to testify."

A large man in a blue gown rose. He described Queen Mary's arrest over implication in the Babington conspiracy, this proved by letters that she had written to that traitor who plotted the death of Her Majesty, the succession of this queen, and the establishment of the Catholic faith in Protestant England.

He got thus far when Mary interrupted. "I wrote no such letters. Any which may be produced are forgeries! As God is my witness, I have never stooped to consider the death of my sister Elizabeth Tudor, nor consented to any plan of it. I have written in favour of her persecuted Catholics, yes. And would be willing to have shed my blood for them, instead of all these years of captivity. But if there were efforts against the life of your monarch, it was without my knowledge. I never met nor dealt with this Babington. Produce these letters, and compare them with *my* hand-writing."

William Cecil now intervened. "These letters are here before us. They may not be in this queen's writing, but in that of her secretaries, Curle and the Frenchman Nau. They prove, in clearest manner, the correspondence between Queen Mary and Anthony Babington, and declare just how Her Majesty Elizabeth was to be put to death. Also they tell of the projected invasion of England by the fleet of Spain, and a Catholic uprising, led by Lord Paget and his brother Charles, to coincide with it—"

"Forgeries! Forgeries!" Mary cried. "Written by *your* servants, to seek to damn me!"

Sir Francis Walsingham, now Secretary of State, announced that there was absolute proof, obtained from one Ballard, a seminary Catholic priest, also John Savage an English squire of that faith, and Thomas Morgan, formerly an agent of Queen Mary, as to her knowledge of Babington's designs, these also declaring that the murder of Queen Elizabeth would be a meritorious action in the sight of God. That the said queen had been excommunicated by the Pope, and that her death was dictated by the Holy Spirit.

Mary burst into tears at this, and sank down with her head on her arms. In consequence the Lord Chancellor decided to adjourn the hearing until the next day.

Somewhat recovered in the morning, Mary, still alone and without any counselling advisers, renewed her protestations that she, as an independent monarch, was nowise under the jurisdiction of this court. She required that this should be recorded.

This gave Cecil and Walsingham pause. They consulted, then declared that they would seek Queen Elizabeth's guidance on this matter of royal jurisdiction. They would prorogue the session meantime and go to Westminster. Queen Mary was to remain captive at Fotheringhay.

Mary was not quite finished even if her captors were. She eyed the entire company, not just its leaders.

"My lords and gentlemen, I place my cause in the hands of God. May He pardon those who have here treated me . . . somewhat rudely!" She even managed a smile at that. "May He keep me from having to do with you all again!"

22

It was on the 25th of the month that the English commissioners met in the Star Chamber at Westminster. They put Mary's servants, Curle and Nau, through an intense examination. The latter bravely asserted that the accusations allegedly made by him against his royal mistress were false, and that his questioners would have to answer to God and all Christian monarchs and the Vatican if, on such wrongous charges, they condemned an innocent princess.

The pair were curtly dismissed.

A parliament was called in London. This unanimously approved of the said commissioners' verdict of Mary's guilt, and petitioned Queen Elizabeth to sentence the Scottish woman to death for high treason, since her speeches had been made in the English kingdom, and contrary to the Protestant religion.

The Tudor considered well. For one crowned monarch to have another executed was almost unheard of, going against all conceptions of royalty and its God-given authority. It was whispered that she would prefer that the accused was secretly assassinated.

Mary was still at Fotheringhay under the harsh control of Sir Amyas Paulet. It was not until 22 November that the Lord Buckhurst arrived there, to announce that Queen Elizabeth had finally been persuaded to promise to sign her acceptance of the execution order, declaring that the will of parliament must prevail, both houses thereof asserting that the Catholic Scots queen's continuing life was incompatible with the security of the Protestant religion.

Offered a Protestant divine to prepare her for death, Mary declined, but requested that she might be granted a Catholic priest's ministrations. This was granted, but only for a very brief meeting and blessing.

Paulet had taken his captor's duties sufficiently seriously to institute a very severe regime at Fotheringhay, to the protests of the two lady-attendants allowed her, although Mary herself accepted it calmly. On one occasion he actually entered her private chamber unannounced, and sat while the queen was still standing, announcing when one of the attending ladies accused him of unbecoming behaviour that since he considered her monarch already dead by law, he saw no fault in it. To emphasise his attitude he then put his hat on, in her presence – which had Mary laughing amusedly, however much her ladies objected.

Servants were whispering about assassination attempts, the Earl of Leicester allegedly advocating this to enable Elizabeth to be spared the accusation of ordering the slaying of a fellow-queen. Mary herself declared that if she was to become a martyr for her faith, it did not greatly concern her how this was achieved.

She wrote her last letter to Elizabeth, in which she announced that she thanked God that He was mercifully about to end her wearisome pilgrimage through this life, and that she looked forward eagerly to the next stage in her progress, nearer to Himself.

However, she asked three favours of Elizabeth Tudor. The first, that her body should be taken to France for interment beside that of her mother, Marie de Guise. The second, that her death should not be secret, but public, in order to emphasise her continuing adherence to the Catholic faith. And third, that her attendants and servants should be free to depart whither they would, on her departure.

She received no answer to these, from Paulet or others.

Belatedly, her cause now came to be supported actively by the Kings of France and Spain, who sent envoys to London urging clemency and the release of the royal prisoner, the former declaring that if he was given charge of Mary Stewart he would ensure that she remained in France and did not seek to promote or organise any efforts to regain her throne or further the Catholic faith in England. Her son, King James, now aged twenty, sent the Master of Gray to London to plead for mercy, he the handsomest man in Europe, allegedly, the plain-featured Elizabeth having a predilection for well-favoured men. However, he had no success on this occasion, notably able as he was, normally, in diplomacy, any more than had the two continental monarchs.

The Tudor at last signed the death-warrants produced by parliament, this on the first day of December 1586. So it was now only a matter of days, after eighteen years of imprisonment.

Mary was ready to go, as she assured her friends, even the harsh Paulet, who only shrugged.

It was on the 7th that the two earls, Shrewsbury and Kent, were ushered into her bedchamber, where she lay in pain with her side after an all but sleepless night, Paulet with them. He it was who read out Elizabeth's warrant of execution, and flatly, the other two looking uncomfortable.

Mary bowed her head and made the sign of the cross. "I thank the good God that this has come, at last," she said. "It is welcome tidings. I shall be happy to leave this world, where I am of little use. I only wish that I had been able to meet, in person, my good sister Elizabeth, and to speak with her in confidence. But this has been refused, and I have been her captive for all these nineteen years, condemned by a tribunal which had no true power over me, for a crime of which I swear, on this Bible, I am innocent. I have never invented, consented, nor pursued any conspiracy for the death of the Queen of England. So, my lords, may I receive the spiritual consolation of a Catholic priest and almoner to prepare me for my end and next beginning?"

Kent shook his head. "The Dean of Peterborough will do what is necessary," he declared.

"But he is not of my faith, a Catholic!" she protested. "I wish no guidance from a Protestant presbyter."

"He you shall have, and no other," she was told.

She inclined her fair head. "When shall I die?" she asked.

"Tomorrow, at eight in the morning."

"Very well. So be it." She drew herself up, in queenly fashion. "You may leave my presence, my lords. And request my ladies to come to me."

Shrewsbury actually bowed out, although Kent did not.

When Mary's ladies came in, they were already in tears.

"Come, come," Mary said, "cease your weeping and lamenting. Rather rejoice, that you see your poor friend so near the end of all her troubles. Dry your eyes, and let us pray together."

That evening, after a supper with her two ladies and her physician, of which none partook very fully, Mary observed, "Did you remark what the Earl of Kent said? That my life would have been the death, and my death would be the life, of their Protestant religion. Oh, how blest I am that here comes the truth. They told me before, falsely, that I was to die because I had plotted against their queen. Now I learn that I am to die for my religion. Here is bliss!"

It was long ere Mary Stewart slept that night, this after writing various letters, one to the Pope, one to her son James, and others to the Kings of France and Spain and to her cousin, Henry of Guise.

Ready as she was to die next morning at this, the beginning of December, it was not to be. Elizabeth hesitated, as well she might, to confirm the sentence, although she had previously signed the warrant and made public proclamation of it. Day after day, week after week, almost all that winter, Mary waited, anticipating the end; and still she was not granted her desire, now, to be done with it all. She besought Fletcher, Dean of Peterborough, to persuade his monarch to act, this to no avail. Even the ladies, much as they loved their royal mistress, prayed that the delay might end; that is, of course, unless Elizabeth's present debating with herself should result, not in further delay – for Mary, after all the years of captivity, fervently sought release from her so sad earthly life – but in a decision to agree to the pleas of the French and Spanish monarchs to take her, and detain her indefinitely in their realms.

Not only Mary and her friends waited and fretted; all England did; likewise Scotland, and the continental kingdoms; this all on one woman's inability to make up her mind, presumably not as to another woman's death but as to when. Had any other monarch in the earth's story had to wait for death in this way? Wait for their last breaths, yes, all being human; but not at the whim of a woman who could not choose just when, not if?

In fact it was 7 February next year, 1587, before there

was decision and the Earls of Shrewsbury and Kent came to Fotheringhay after midday dinner and demanded audience with the Queen of Scots. She sent them word that she was indisposed and in her bed; but that if the matter was of consequence she would rise and receive them. Their reply that they would brook no delay got them admittance and, conducted to her bedchamber, they found her seated at a small table beside the bed. Gracious as ever, she greeted them, and inclined her head when they declared that Her Majesty, *their* queen, overcome by the importunity of her subjects, had at last given orders for Mary's execution, for which these two had brought the warrant.

Inclining her head, Mary waited.

Paulet, with them, then read the commission, in his usual abrupt manner.

She listened, without interrupting, grim as it was, and then bowed her head and made the sign of the cross, asserting quietly that she thanked her gracious God for sending her the release of death, to leave this world where she was of no use; and that she judged it a signal happiness that she should be dying for the Holy Catholic and Apostolic Church.

That evening, left with her ladies, after supper Mary called for a cup of wine, and drank to all who loved her, begging them to drink to her further journey nearer to Christ. This they did, on their knees, with tears. She declared to them that her personal wardrobe was sorely depleted; but she selected what was left of it, to give to these her good friends as keepsakes. Also such jewellery as she had managed to retain – that is, all save the celebrated string of black pearls, from Scotland's River Tay, these on a gold chain which she tended to wear entwined in her hair, the only such reputedly in all the world, black pearls being rare indeed and so many as forty unique. These, her especial pride, she would retain as her endeared link with her native land until the last. Pearls were the symbol of perfection, and only persons of the highest rank permitted by tradition to wear them. So be it. She would carry them with her to the scaffold.

It was two in the morning, that last night, before she washed her feet and went to lie on her bed, her lips moving in prayer. She was to die at eight, so she would rise at six. She doubted whether she would sleep – after all, she would have ample opportunity for sleeping hereafter! Although, perhaps not? Was not the next life too precious for sleeping in? She did not undress, clad now in black with a white veil.

Four hours later a messenger came to announce that the lords were awaiting her. Mary concluded her prayers, not hastening. The sheriff entered, with his white staff, to conduct her out, her physician pleading with her to take a little of bread and wine, as her last meal, fearing for her exhaustion. Smiling, she thanked him, saying that she wished that it was the bread and wine of the Mass, and she raised up before him the little ivory crucifix which was never far from her, kissing it.

Her attendants and servants tearfully were for accompanying her to the great hall of the castle where she was to die, but were turned back by the sheriff, save for two ladies and Sir Andrew Melville her steward and master of the household. To them she gave her last message.

"Weep not, my friends. And tell my son James that I have done nothing which may prejudice his kingdom of Scotland."

So, with only these three, she was led to the scaffold, which had been erected at the far end on a raised platform only two feet in height and covered with a black cloth, on it the block and three seats, one with a cushion.

Mounting this without the least evident distress, Mary went to sit on the cushioned chair, as though it were a throne, her ladies to stand behind her, while Shrewsbury and Kent sat on the other two seats, and the sheriff led the Dean Fletcher, Paulet and the Clerk of the Privy Council to stand. The hall in front of them was crowded, some two hundred having gathered to witness this extraordinary occasion, the slaying of a monarch.

Mary, facing all, spoke out, and clearly. "I testify, before this company that, despite my rights as a sovereign princess, which have been invaded and trampled on, I thank God that now I die as a Catholic worshipper; and innocent of any plot or consent to any practice against Queen Elizabeth's life. I accuse no one. But when I am gone, much will be discovered which is now hid, and the objects of those who have procured my death will be disclosed to the world."

Dean Fletcher came and prayed for her soul, in the Protestant fashion, she shaking her head but adding an Amen, and repeating a brief excerpt from a psalm in the Latin at the end.

Kent, noting her holding the little crucifix before her, urged that she should renounce such antiquated superstitions, declaring that the image of Christ served little purpose if she had not Him engraved on her heart.

"Ah," she returned, "there is nothing more becoming for a dying Christian to carry than this remembrance of His suffering and redemption. Impossible it is to have such in my hand, and keep my heart unmoved." She kissed the cross. "As Thine arms were spread, oh my God, out upon the cross, so receive me within those arms, of Thy mercy. Extend Thy pity and forgive my sins."

Her two ladies were ordered to remove the queen's upper robe, so that only her red satin bodice covered her fine breasts. The executioner, by the name of Bull, embarrassedly introduced himself, muttering apologies. She greeted him kindly, declaring that she held no grudge against him, he only to do what his masters ordered – and smilingly added that she had never been used to *male* grooms of the chamber, nor to undressing before so many people!

Then she turned to her ladies. "My dear and faithful friends, and companions," she said, her voice now quavering, "with me to the last. Here is my final token of love." And raising both hands, she carefully removed from her hair the circlet of black pearls on a golden chain which she wore on especial occasions, to lift and hang it round the neck of one. "Keep these always, none other to have them. Take them back to Scotland, where they came from, my last gift on this earth, whatever we may exchange, one day, in the next!"

The recipient was too overcome to speak.

Jane Kennedy was ordered to blindfold the queen with a white sash, brought for that purpose.

Mary sat down on the cushion again. She held herself upright, head high, and murmured a prayer. She had anticipated that she would be executed in the French fashion, with sword slashing throat. But now Bull, more unhappy than ever, declared that he had his orders to use an axe. Would Her Majesty kneel?

So Mary had to remove that bandage, and consider the block before her, and how she would get down and place her head so that her neck was outstretched and bare for the axe, Paulet curtly directing her. She made the sign of the cross.

But, stammering, Bull had to point out that all was not quite right and ready. Laying her head thus, the axe-blade would descend partly on the wood. Her Majesty would have to move forward somewhat and stretch out her neck, to give him a clear stroke. Would she be so kind?

She edged on a little, as directed, and bent again, saying clearly, "Into Thy hands I commit my spirit, oh Lord of love, for Thou hast redeemed me." This to the wails of her ladies.

But still her position was evidently not exactly right for the desired fall of the axe, desired by Bull at least; and she had to dispose herself slightly otherwise, this while Paulet tutted and the women agonised.

Even now the axeman was not quite satisfied. And advisedly. For when at last he raised his weapon high and brought it down in swinging force, the blade partly struck against wood and thus slanted on to the bandaged head, rather than the neck.

The queen gasped out her last two words, "Sweet Jesus!" and then was silent, evidently stunned.

Which was as well, for the next blow broke her neck, but only half detached head from body, and had to be severed once again.

Lips continued to move – but Mary Stewart was dead, and thankfully.

Stooping and laying aside the bloody axe, Bull lifted up the head by the hair, and called, "God save the queen!"

And, that all there realised which queen he prayed for, Dean Fletcher loudly exclaimed, "So let all Queen Elizabeth's enemies perish!"

Only one Amen sounded for that, coming from the Earl of Kent.

The Queen of Scots had reached heaven's gate, at forty-four years – and had been captive for nineteen of them.

EPILOGUE

Lord Talbot, Shrewsbury's son, was sent to gallop the long way from Fotheringhay, in Northamptonshire, to Greenwich, where Elizabeth was waiting; and he later recounted how, when he informed her of the execution, she after a moment's thought received it with assumed indignation, declaring that she was devastated, overcome with grief, and would wear weeds of mourning, this however not convincing the young man. And she had swung on her secretary, Davison, alleging that she had only signed that death-warrant for safety's sake, for him to hold on to and not to use. She even went so far as to send the unfortunate Davison to the Tower for a period of imprisonment, and fined him ten thousand pounds, to his ruin, in her strange play-acting, poor man, blaming all on him and her Council.

Nevertheless, she ordered London to rejoice. Bells rang out, bonfires were lit, and there was feasting and merriment in the streets, in celebration of the final end of a so-called menace to the nation. Paulet was made a Knight of the Garter.

Mary's body was embalmed and placed in a lead coffin, but was not given burial, remaining walled up at Fotheringhay, not sent to France for interment as she had so earnestly requested.

Elizabeth Tudor was a very strange woman.

In France, Mary was mourned and hailed as a martyr for

the Catholic faith. In Scotland there was anger, with young King James ordering that all communication with England must cease, however little he and his advisers had done to save his mother.

The corpse remained unburied from February until July, when at last it was transported to Peterborough Cathedral. It remained there until 1603, when at last James ascended Elizabeth's throne, and had his mother's coffin transferred to Westminster Abbey.

The end of a sorry song.

HISTORICAL NOTE

The keen historian may consider that some liberties have been taken on dates and occurrences in this story. But they, more than anyone, will know that the history books can differ widely in their accounts of events and, when telling a story, such as this is, the facts as reported variously must be woven in with as much accuracy as is consistent with a believable tale. The author hopes he will be forgiven.